SKYROCKET STEELE

SKYROCKET STEELE

RON GOULART

WILDSIDE PRESS

SKYROCKET STEELE

Published by:
Wildside Press
P.O. Box 301
Holicong, PA 18928-0301
www.wildsidepress.com

First Wildside Press edition: 2003

1

The war was going to start in less than a year.

Franklin Delano Roosevelt had just begun his third term as President, Joe Louis had just knocked out a heavyweight pushover named Abe Simon. After a lull, the Luftwaffe was resuming its firebombing of London. Charles Lindbergh was getting ready to address a big America First rally in Chicago and Congress, after much debate and haggling, passed the Lend-Lease Bill. The "Pot o' Gold" radio show, in spite of its handsome $1,000 prize, was sinking in the Hooper ratings. Bob Hope, Kate Smith, "The Path to Love," and the Aldrich Family were doing fine. Hitler, the world's best-known vegetarian, was planning his spring campaign. Emperor Hirohito decided this was the year to annex all of southern Asia. Mussolini, another vegetarian, was celebrating his eighteenth anniversary as dictator of Italy amid rumors he was dying of syphilis. Boris Karloff was wowing Broadway in *Arsenic and Old Lace*. Gypsy Rose Lee, noted stripper, got a divorce. So did magician Blackstone, noted for his floating-lady illusion. A man named Joseph Lyman was granted a patent for something called radar.

It was a splendid spring night in Hollywood, warmed by a pleasant wind coming from the inland desert. Looking up through the leaves of the real, green palm trees, you could see a clear black sky rich with stars. From down at the Garden of Allah the sound of beautiful golden-haired actresses splashing in the big swimming pool came drifting, along with the sound of someone playing Cole Porter tunes on a piano with one dead key.

The front of the Club Zig Zag was all gleaming chrome panels decorated with flashes of ebony lightning. Tiny planted floodlights illuminated the miniature trees lining the white gravel pathway leading from the crowded parking lot to the wide silver door of the night spot. It looked even better than a Los Angeles funeral parlor.

The handsome door flapped open and Errol Flynn came out, grinning, wiping lipstick off his left cheek. He hesitated, swaying gently from side to side. He tilted his head, listening.

A block away a newsboy was shouting. "Extra . . . bomb . . . hundreds die . . . extra . . ."

You couldn't make it all out.

Flynn shrugged, stepped onto the white gravel path. A top-down Buick convertible, bright lemon yellow, swooped down and stopped. A lovely Chinese girl, clad in a suit of red silk pajamas, leaned across and opened the passenger door. Flynn, stumbling, got in. The yellow car gunned off, heading for Sunset.

"It doesn't fit," complained Pete Tinsley.

"It fits, it fits—trust me," said Hix. "It fits adequately. You look absolutely swell."

They were standing just beyond the spot where Flynn had been, the dust of his swift departure settling on them.

"One shoulder is way up here," said Pete. "I look like I'm always on the brink of shrugging."

Hix pushed open the door of the nightclub, tugging Pete inside with him. They passed the hat-check room, in front of which a drunken Army colonel was trying on top hats which didn't fit.

"Come on, now, smile," urged Hix. "Act employed."

The lanky light-haired young man frowned. "I ought to be home working on that new novelette for *Stimulating Science Stories* instead of—"

"After tonight you can kiss off those cheapo markets. You are on the threshold of a bright new . . . Hey, there's Hedda Hopper, way over there. Hi, Hedda." Hix squinted. "I didn't quite catch what Hedda said by way of reply."

"Sounded like 'Up yours, Hix.'"

Scowling Hix brushed at the lapel of his dinner jacket. He was a moderate-sized man, fuzzy-haired and thirty-one. "What would motivate Hedda to say 'Up yours' to a screenwriter of my standing? Unless she's uneasy about that last item I gave her for her column, concerning my romance with Joan Blondell."

"You're not having any romance with Joan Blondell."

"Which could be what prompts Hedda Hopper to cry 'Up yours, Hix' smack dab in the middle of one of Hollywood's flashiest rendezvous . . . There's Ralph Bellamy over by the bandstand. Hi, pal. You were great in *Footsteps in the Dark*. Notice, Peter, how his tux doesn't fit much better than yours."

"That's why he never gets the girl," said Pete. "And his suit doesn't have bullet holes in it."

"Neither does yours. We got all those patched up, damn it, and there is absolutely not a thing to fret over."

"My back is chilly. I'm starting to suspect some of them have come unsewed."

The thirteen-piece band, every man in spotless white tie and white tails, was midway through a dreamy version of "Blue Moon." The dance floor was packed with cheek-to-cheek couples.

"There's Dennis O'Keefe over there with Bert Wheeler and Billy Gilbert. O'Keefe's a cinch to hit it big."

"Next time you borrow a suit from your studio, Hix, see if you can—"

"You got—trust me—the only damn tux I could swipe from wardrobe on such short notice." Hix took hold of his elbow. "One of the batch they were just using in *Chinatown Murders*. What have you got on your hair?"

Pete scratched at his sand-colored hair. "Oh, I know what you're smelling. It's ketchup from this suit. They must have used it for blood."

"Naw, they don't use ketchup out at Star-Spangled Studios."

"Well, something with tomatoes in it."

"Hi, Lupe. You're looking just terrific. That was Lupe Velez. No undies—did you notice?" Hix kept leading him deeper into the crowd.

"I noticed. All writers are observant," Pete said. "But we're kidding ourselves, Hix—this isn't going to work."

"Sure it's going to work, kiddo—it's a cinch. Trust me, Pete, you are on the brink of something big."

"Yeah, like a precipice."

"Listen, you're how old now? Twenty-seven, twenty-eight?"

"Twenty-eight."

"Been out here in sun-kissed California for three long years and you still don't have one damn screen credit. No, you drone away in the Laguna Vista Apartment Court, pulling down a penny a goddamn word from Manhattan pulps such as *Stimulating Science, Overwhelming Western,* and *Devastating Terror,* while—"

"*Overwhelming Western* has upped me to two cents."

"I'm offering you, for Christ sake, a chance to break out of your fetters, to get into the movie racket. Here's a golden opportunity to work with a seasoned screenwriter on a major script."

"I thought this was a serial."

"A *major* serial. And I'm going to get you a hundred fifty dollars a week—a whole twenty-five smackers better than the Guild minimum."

"I'm not used to being paid by weeks instead of words."

"There's Charlie Ruggles. Hiya, Charlie, old buddy." Hix waved. "It's time for you to break loose, brother. You've got talent, Pete—a terrific imagination. That opening you did on 'Vampires of the Venusian Void' was swell, the work of a born genius."

Pete said, "I still don't think even a producer like Milton Owls is going to be interested in a pulp magazine hack."

"Listen, pal, hordes of absolutely brilliant screenwriters have graduated from the cheesy pages of the pulpwoods. Dashiell Hammett, for instance. And look where he is today."

"I think I saw him sprawled flat on his face in front of the bar."

"Hi, Chester. You were beautiful in *Meet Boston Blackie*. Notice that one shoulder of his tux was higher than the other."

"He was shrugging."

"Ah, our goal at long last." Hix rubbed his fuzzy head.

"Maybe we ought to phone Owls at the studio instead of—"

"Hooey—too much red tape even for me to cut. This is better—trust me. When I heard he was going to hit this joint tonight, I knew it was absolutely the right way to . . . Here's the very guy you're looking for, Milt."

"Which guy?" Milton Owls was a hefty man, fifty-three, squat and wide, wearing gold-rimmed spectacles. He took these off, blinking, and breathed on the lenses before wiping them with his crisp white table napkin.

"The Mars guy I was telling you about," explained Hix.

Pete was noticing the pretty, slim auburn-haired girl who sat next to the producer. She was young, not more than twenty-one, wearing a simple white satin evening gown. Smiling up at Pete, she said, "Hit him for two-hundred bucks a week."

The other man at the table was too large for his tux. "Dames shouldn't talk money," he remarked, scowling, thick bushy brows tapping together.

Owls fitted his glasses back on. "So you know all about Mars?"

"Well, I've written about the planet quite a lot, yeah."

"Shit, I bet he don't even know where Mars is," said the large shaggy man.

Sitting down uninvited, Pete pointed at the ceiling. "Mars is up there." He offered his hand to the girl. "I'm Pete Tinsley."

"Tracy Flinn." She shook his hand; her skin was smooth and warm. "With an *I* in the middle."

"A fresh guy maybe," observed Owls.

"A wiseass," said the big man. "We ought maybe to give him the bum's rush."

Clearing his throat, Hix settled into the only vacant chair. "Peter Tinsley is a man of science, Thompson. Naturally, a guy such as yourself, wrapped up in being a top-notch assistant producer out at Star-Spangled, you—"

"Could you honestly help Hix write this goddamn thing?" Owls asked Pete.

"The serial, you mean?"

"Sure he can," Hix said. "That's why I'm telling you you got to hire him to assist me on the script, Milt. You know damn well, after the terrific job I did on *Guns of the Purple Rider* and *Six Golden Scorpions,* that—"

"Only five this schmuck puts in," said Owls, chuckling. "A great script mind, but sloppy. We get to where we're shooting the last chapter, Chapter Twelve, of *Six Golden Scorpions,* out on location near the frigging Springs, and Isaac says to me . . . You know Isaac Simplicissimus? Great director for a kraut. Anyhow, he says to me, "Mildon, I chust realize, ve got only fife dodgosted scorpions. Und not siggs.' Jesus, we had to haul this bum Hix out of some bordello down in Caliente to write in one more goddamn scorpion."

"Tell him," said Hix with a frown, "what that particular chapter play grossed."

Thompson muttered, "It didn't do so bad."

"Republic would love a serial that grossed like *Six Golden Scorpions,*" Hix said, voice rising. "Columbia would dance up and down. Hell, Louis B. Mayer might think about teaming Clark Gable and Vivian Leigh again if he could get a script that terrific. 'Hix, come on over to MGM and you need provide us no more than five scorpions, my boy. Make it four. But get over here damn fast, so we can start stuffing your pockets with dough.' I hear, matter of fact, Mayer's looking for a hot property for Tracy and Hepburn. Maybe I'll—"

"Such a wise guy." Owls chuckled once more. "This goddamn thing takes place on Mars," he said in Pete's direction. "You could handle that?"

"Sure, I just finished a novel about Mars called 'Warrior Queen of the Red Planet,'" Pete replied. "It'll be coming out in *Thrilling Wond*—"

"Title stinks," said Owls. "What do you think, Thompson?"

The large man grunted. "Can't have queen in it— people will think it's about pansies," he said. "Put red in the title, they figure it's a Bolshie flick."

Pete was watching the girl once more. "You work at Star-Spangled, too?"

"She's his secretary." Thompson pointed his thick thumb at the girl and then at the fat Owls. "Private secretary."

"I don't know, Hix." Owls sighed. "We got to start shooting in six, seven weeks. I absolutely got to have a scenario in two weeks and the whole frigging script in no more than five. My publicity people are already howling my production crew is having fits." He cocked his head at Pete. "Like the title?"

"Which title?"

"For the goddamn serial."

Hix said, leaning an elbow on the tabletop, "I told you back at your place, remember? It's going to be called *Skyrocket Steele*."

"Terrific title," said Pete. "Would you people actually pay me two hundred a week?"

"If I did I'd have to cut Hix. He's already holding me up for three hundred."

"You want quality, you have to pay for it," reminded Hix. "Hey, there's Ginger Rogers. Hi, redhead. That can't be Fritz Henzler she's dancing with, is it?"

"That bastard," said Owls, snarling. "Him and his frigging German-American Horseman League. They ought to put him on a boat and ship him back to the Nazis."

Tracy asked Pete, "Did you hear about the latest raid on London?"

"Hix barged in when the news was coming on," he said. "Worse than usual?"

"Supposed to be the roughest Nazi strike yet." She nodded, long auburn hair brushing her bare tanned shoulders. "I'm really worried England isn't going to be able to hang on."

"Screw England," said Owls. "They never understood Star-Spangled's best pictures over there. Wouldn't even book *The Singing Bellhop*. Anybody who don't understand tenors, who needs 'em. I'll give you a hundred fifty, kid."

"You better take it," advised Hix. "You can't expect to pull down what a seasoned writer gets the first crack off the reel." His hair had become fuzzier and wilder.

Pete said, "Okay, I accept." Owls offered his plump hand. "Come on out to the studio tomorrow with Hix. We'll sign some papers, then you can get cracking. I got to have something for my people goddamn quick."

"Would you," Tracy asked, "like to dance with me, Pete?"

"Yep, I would indeed." He stood and went around to her side of the white table. "I'll . . . oops! Stepped on your wrap."

Tracy smiled, getting up. "No, that was the chimpanzee."

Glancing down, Pete confirmed it was a dozing chimp he'd put his foot on. "Yours?"

"Oh, no, he belongs to Hunneker. You know, he makes the jungle man movies for MGM. He insists on dragging the poor thing along with him when he's on the town, but then he gets to drinking or gambling and Toko is left stranded." She bent to stroke the slumbering animal behind an ear. "Toko, for some unexplained reason, is very fond of me." Taking Pete's hand, she guided him toward the immense circular ebony dance floor.

The band had just started playing "String of Pearls."

"Be easier to go over this way."

"I want to avoid June Maze's table. Know her?"

"No, but I've seen her in a couple movies Hix wrote."

"She'll be in *Skyrocket Steele*. She's okay, for a top-heavy nitwit, but those guys she pals around with . . ."

"That's right, she's supposed to be the girlfriend of Gypsy Shuster, the alleged mobster."

"She is, and there's nothing alleged about Gypsy. He's a fully accredited hoodlum and . . . oh, damn!"

"Hey, you told me you wasn't dancing." A big curly-haired man had left the June Maze party to come pushing over to

Tracy's side. "Yet that don't seem to be the case." He gripped her bare arm.

"Ease off, Dime," the girl advised, attempting to free herself from him.

Dime Gallardo grinned. "We'll have us a couple dances, long as they don't play any more of that South American crapola. Then we can sit out a few in the—"

"Let her go." Pete clapped his hand over that of the mobster. There were a lot of big rings and bigger knuckles.

Dime ignored him. "We going to dance or ain't we, Trace?"

"I don't want to tangle with you in the middle of this damn place," Pete told him. "But I will if you don't turn her loose right now."

Very slowly, Dime took in Pete. Then he laughed. Snorting, he pushed the girl away. "Okay, jerk, we'll tangle private. Then, while you're picking your keester up off the linoleum, I'll get back to my girl." He jerked a finger in Tracy's direction. "Wait right here, honey."

"Pete, you don't have to—"

"Let's go sucker." Dime grabbed hold of Pete's shoulder.

The borrowed suit made some odd new ripping noises. "Damn, there go more of the bullet holes."

Dime, laughing in anticipation, tugged Pete across the ebony dance floor, around the ivory bandstand and into a shadowy corridor. "This'll do fine," he announced. "I decked a couple other punks here once."

He flat-handed Pete's chest.

The force of the shove was such that it caused Pete to smack the opposite wall. The collision shook the plaster walls; the one dim orange-bulbed overhead lamp jittered; all of Pete's teeth and bones rattled.

"You ain't going to dance no more." Hunched, massive arms swinging, Dime came stalking for Pete.

Pete was having considerable trouble getting several body functions—ones he'd assumed were fully automatic—to work. His breathing was choppy, irregular, threatening to shut off. His vision was furry and he had the impression his left eye was blinking twice as fast as his right.

But he had to meet Dime's charge. Biting at the air, struggling to breath in some at least halfway normal way, he willed his eyes to show him the approaching hood more clearly.

"Fun," Dime was murmuring, "this is going to be fun."

"Up yours," gasped Pete, borrowing from Hedda Hopper. Holding on to his balance as best he could, he swung a fist in the general direction of Dime.

The punch barely reached the big man's chest. Dime, however, gave a sudden surprised shout and went rising up to the ceiling. His head smacked the dappled plaster very hard, causing his jaw to snap shut with a bony crunch. Dime seemed to hesitate up there a few seconds before plummeting down. He slammed into the floor, groaned, spilled out like wax melting.

Shaking his head, Pete backed away from the unconscious man. Three more steps and he was aware Tracy was standing in the corridor. He put an arm around the girl, partly out of growing affection and partly to keep from falling over. "I didn't do that to him, Tracy—make him jump that way," he said. "I hardly, I don't think, hit the guy at all. You must have done it . . . but how could you? He flew all the way to the ceiling . . . you didn't even touch him."

"Never mind, Pete," suggested Tracy. "Forget this and what you think maybe you saw. I couldn't let him hurt you, okay?"

"Yeah, sure, but how the—"

"Forget it, please." She twisted, pressed against him and kissed him. After a while she said again, "Forget."

"Okay," he promised, "I'll forget."

2

Out of its oval cloth speaker the table radio was saying, ". . . repeat that. The British Embassy flatly denies reports that Winston Churchill was seriously injured in last night's devastating German bombing raid of London. And now we return you to "The Path to Love," already in progress."

". . . and who is this strange and haunting girl Lord Brett met so unexpectedly last evening in New York City's fashionable Swan Club? Can she have some connection with the amnesia of the still missing Charles Sutterford? Can Lord Brett afford to trust her with the dismal secret he harbors? We'll find out in just one minute, right after we visit with Aunt Betty in her spotless Super Lard kitchen, where she is about to give the always hungry young Denny her recipe for peach cobbler . . ."

Pete, mentally tuning out the broadcast, picked up one of his yellow dime-store tablets. He selected a fresh pencil from the scatter of them beside him on the faded bed quilt. After a few tentative bites at the eraser end, he commenced writing.

. . . a shadow of deeper intensity took shape in the underworld alley. Had there been an observer in this bleak corner of criminal hell on that particular dismal 3 A.M., he would have . . .

"Nope, *dismal*'s not quite the right word," Pete decided, erasing.

. . . that particular fog-shrouded 3 A.M., he would have Tracy . . .

That last word Pete found himself doodling in the margin. Dropping the pad and pencil, he stretched his arms up over his head. It was a little after ten and he was sitting cross-legged on the wall bed of his small apartment. A bright golden morning glowed on the other side of his windows, hidden somewhat by the stiff yellowing lace curtains.

"She didn't use jujitsu or anything like that on Dime Gallardo," he said to himself. "Hell, she never got closer than five feet to the son of a bitch."

After eyeing the peach-colored stucco ceiling for a moment, Pete selected a different notebook and a new pencil.

. . . halfbreeds, the lot of them. Leering now in the sooty light of the dismal adobe hut in which Laughin' Jim of the Texas

Rangers . . .

"Damn, there's dismal again."

. . . the musky adobe hut in which Laughin' Jim, the lightning-quick Texas Ranger, found himself . . .

Pete dropped the story he was fashioning for *Alarming West*. He unwound his long legs, swung off the bed. Then he made a quick backward dive, smacking the rising bed with both hands to keep it from going back up into the wall. He crossed the flower-bordered rug to gaze out the window at the morning street.

The midgets who lived in the apartment court across the way were playing touch football around the cockeyed birdbath. The freckled kid who delivered the *Los Angeles Times* was using a beat-up old red wagon today.

Hix was not approaching in any direction.

"Fifteen minutes late." Sitting on the bed again, Pete selected a new tablet and pencil.

. . . that particularly dismal heat which only the jungles of Venus can produce engulfed . . .

"Shit, dismal!" He left the bed, not caring that it rose two feet. He slumped into the sprung, mateless sofa chair and locked his hands behind his head.

The radio caught his attention again. Lord Brett, in his clipped British accent, was arguing with someone.

"And I tell you, man, amnesia isn't contagious."

"I've never seen you so nervous, Lord Brett. It's almost as though you've had some tremendous shock."

"Well, Dr. Henry, I did meet a rather unusual young woman last evening at Manhattan's most fashionable . . ."

After snapping the radio off, Pete grabbed the latest issue of *Dime Detective* from the lopsided end table. The lead novelette failed to hold his attention and he tossed the pulp magazine aside.

Sometimes, when he shut his eyes, he could see the Flinn girl quite clearly. Sometimes not at all. "How the hell did she make that bastard jump? All the way up to the—"

"The funniest thing."

Pete opened his eyes. Boots McKay, the girl from the next apartment, had pushed open his unlockable door and was standing on the threshold. "What, Boots?"

"When I awakened," the pretty brunette said, "I noticed an ape staring in the window at me."

"Probably one of the midgets."

"I've been in show business since I was six, Pete. I know a chimp from a midget." Boots, in a white sailor-style dress, came into the room. "He was sitting out in the flower box, picking my geraniums and stuffing them into his little hairy nostrils. He very much resembled that dopey chimp in the Hunneker films."

"Toko!" Pete popped up, started toward the doorway. "Don't tell me he followed me home."

"Relax, the little schmuck is long gone. Last time I saw him he was swinging from the telephone poles and heading for La Cienega." Boots settled down on his bed, crossing her long handsome legs. "This is a very strange town. I bet you sometimes miss Youngstown, Ohio."

"I was never in Youngstown, Ohio—not once. I'm from East Moline, Illinois." He returned to the window, checking again for the overdue Hix. An old man in a tan coat-sweater and pin-stripe suit trousers was going by carrying a sign championing some new crackpot pension plan.

"Tell me about the brawl you were in last night at the Zig Zag," Boots requested. "I don't have much time because I've got an interview with Busby Berkeley's third in command. About a feature spot in a new musical."

"Congratulations. It wasn't a brawl, though, Boots—only me and some other fellow. Technically that isn't really a brawl. See, I've written quite a lot for *Stimulating Fight Stories* so I know—"

"This guy I'm due to see, and he's supposed to be just about Busby Berkeley's right or left hand, noticed me in my last three pics, he told me."

"Even when you were a dancing egg in the Feather Your Nest number in *Varsities of 1941?*"

Boots's eyelashes fluttered. "He recognized my legs sticking out," she explained. "He says Busby Berkeley himself asked him to screen my portion of the big production number from *Hot Tamales on Broadway*."

"The one where you're a dancing light bulb in the Electrical Progress Ballet?"

"No, you're thinking of *Hot Tamales Get Married*. In *Hot*

Tamales on Broadway I was the featured carrot in the Garden of Love number. I came on right after Alan Jones finds out Lupe Velez is only the cook at that ritzy Park Ave mansion and not a deb at all."

"I remember—we saw the picture together," said Pete as he made another inspection of the street.

A yellow tour bus was rolling by. It said, "Here you see, folks, scampering in their familiar prankish way almost into our path, the famous Hermansdorfer Midgets. You all remember their cavorting so delightfully with Jane Withers in . . ."

"I hear tell," said Boots, moistening her fingertip and rubbing at a tiny spec on her knee, "you're going to work out at Star-Spangled. That's swell."

"Yep, I'll be collaborating with Hix."

"Hix." Boots made a raspberry sound. "I wouldn't trust that jerk any further than I could toss Grauman's Chinese—"

"Aha, is this truly Boots McKay I see before me?" Hix, clad in a fuchsia-colored polo shirt and desert-brown slacks, came bounding in out of the morning. "That is you, is it not? I'm unused to seeing you out of your shell."

"I hear Hedda Hopper told you where you could stick it last night," remarked the brunette dancer.

Hix, shoulders slightly hunched, was studying her lovely legs. "I can envision a terrific horror fillum with you, my dear. We get Lionel Atwill, maybe toss in Basil Rathbone for good measure. These two lads attempt to graft those terrific gams of yours onto another body—or could be just a new head would be sufficient." Hix slowly circled the peach-toned room. "Then we cut to a tight closeup as they open your skull. 'What do you think of that, Lionel, old chap?' 'Jove, it's amazing, Basil, old bean!' We go in tighter for a glimpse of your brain and there 'tis . . . a little dried up pea. 'How do you suppose the poor wench reached the age of twenty-six with naught but a little teenie-weenie pea rattling around inside her sconce, Lionel?' 'It bloody well beggars explanation, Basil, old dear, although—'"

"Save your wisecracks for your crummy B movies, Hix." The girl gathered herself together, left the bed, and crossed to the door, "Don't let this moron screw you up with Star-Spangled, Pete."

"Good luck with Busby Berkeley."

Watching the dancer exit, Hix said, "Not *the* Busby Berkeley? I heard he was on the skids, but didn't think he'd sunk low enough to audition the likes of—"

"I didn't notice your car drive up."

"We'll use your jalopy," Hix informed him. "I hooked a ride over here with Niles Pomerene, the great silent star."

"Didn't see his car either."

"Niles is piloting the star tour bus," said Hix. "He made a slight detour for me. Good thing those little midget assholes were cavorting around outside here, because we had a busload of tourists who were commencing to wonder what famed Hollywood luminary could possibly live in such a sleazy neighborhood. Did you hear what a bunch of those little buggers tried to do with Jane Withers?"

"Yeah." Pete gathered a few pencils off the patchwork bedspread and dropped them in a side pocket of the sport coat he'd slipped into. "Let's get going."

"A few more deals such as this one, my boy, and you can leave sleazy neighborhoods behind. It'll be goodbye to all this. No more tackiness, no more pea-brain hoofers, no more pulpy potboilers."

"We'll see," said Pete.

3

Pete's blue '36 Plymouth coupe crested a hill and was now within a mile of the new Star-Spangled Studios in Burbank.

The late morning street was lined with stately palm trees. The pretty girls in their bright spring dresses all looked liked movie stars or potential movie stars. The men—even those in uniform—gave the impression they were all tanned and handsome and just waiting for the one big break that would catapult them to stardom. All the older people—the housewives in their print dresses and the retired gentlemen in their mismatched double-breasted suits—had faces rich with character. The shops and restaurants had a new, expectant aura. There was a juice stand occupying a giant aluminum orange, a sandwich shop shaped like a huge crouching frog, and a radio store with a mock console phonograph a good ten feet tall blaring on the sidewalk in front of it. A market run by a man in a farmer's straw hat promised Valley Fresh Produce; a secondhand bookshop had festoons of bright pulp magazines decorating its dust-free front windows. At the corner a fifty-year-old newsboy, who always kept his three fat Jean Harlow scrapbooks in his kiosk, was quoting President Roosevelt in a loud, husky voice.

"He owns it?" Pete was asking.

"Lock, stock, and barrel, so rumor has it."

"I didn't know Clifford Klaus was interested in movies," said Pete. "I thought he was entirely devoted to business machines and electrical supplies."

"His vast millions flow in from many sources, one of which is apparently Star-Spangled Studios." Hix was slouched in the passenger seat, scanning the street. He whistled appreciatively when a girl in a multicolor sarong went by on an English bicycle. "By the way, you ought to ease Boots out of your life, old pal. I had a wife much like her once—terrific from her toes up to about here. She burned with the gemlike ambition to front her own all-girl orchestra, which aggregation she felt I ought to finance with—"

"What can you tell me about Tracy Flinn?" His fingers tapped on the one-arm-driver knob on the steering wheel.

"Well, she doesn't know how to spell Flynn. Otherwise the lass seems bright, intelligent, and kind." He shifted position on the imitation-leather seat. "Frankly, Pete, you ought to be watchful with a dame who seems too honest and sweet."

"I like her, though."

"Well, don't let that fondness lead you into any further fracases with the likes of Dime Gallardo and Gypsy Shuster," the fuzzy-haired writer advised. "A lot of the crap you see in gangster movies really does happen to people. You don't want to find yourself getting worked over with a baseball bat or wading in the Santa Monica surf with cement shoes. Next time you encounter Gallardo, see if you can refrain from beating up the bastard."

"I didn't actually . . . never mind."

"Didn't actually what?"

"Nothing. I haven't figured it all out yet. Skip it."

Pete braked the coupe, causing several rattling sounds to occur. The wrought-iron gates of the studio were now only five feet from the front fenders.

The Star-Spangled Studios covered thirty walled-in acres, brand new salmon-colored buildings and sound stages, with bright red tile roofs. There was an abundance of flower-bordered paths, enough palm trees for a Hunneker film.

"Billy's on the gate—good." Leaning out his window, Hix casually saluted the plump uniformed guard. "Howdy, William, me lad. 'Tis I, the celebrated Hix. This is my new and gifted partner, the equally brilliant Peter Tinsley."

The old man peered out of his guard hut into the sunny morning. "That wouldn't be the same Pete Tinsley who writes those yarns in *Stimulating Cowboy* magazine?"

"This is indeed he," said Hix.

"Tell him he don't know his fanny from his elbow when it comes to cows. He put the wrong kind in . . ." They lost the rest of the critique when Billy stepped back inside his hut to punch the gate release.

"You're making a name for yourself," remarked Hix.

"He must mean 'Rusty Rides South' in last month's *Stimulating Cowboy*." Pete drove onto the studio grounds, savoring it a little. "You read that one over, claimed it had the true tang of the Old West."

"So? What's tang got to do with cows? I don't know a Hereford from a Dalmatian."

"Dalmatians have spots."

"With that kind of knowledge, you ought to switch to *Stimulating Dog Stories*. Turn off onto Road J— we'll stick this buggy in the writers' lot."

Pete complied, swerving to avoid a procession of mounted and fierce-looking desert tribesmen. "You mean you wrote *Guns of the Purple Rider* without knowing anything about cattle?"

"Action is my specialty, not animals. I wrote that same story two or three times, in fact. Hey, look at that Alfa Romeo over in the next lot. Belongs to that bum, Thompson. And take a gander at Wally Reisberson's Cord. Wally pulls down fifty thousand dollars per annum just for writing scripts. Gives us both something to aim at, Pietro." Hix bounced out of the car. "Yeah, I used the Purple Rider plot here at Star-Spangled and I did it as *Secret of the Masked Horseman* over at Republic in 1937 or thereabouts. Boots would've loved that version. The villain went around wearing an enormous golden idol's head. He didn't dance much, and yet—"

"You better tell me a little more about *Skyrocket Steele*." Climbing out of his coupe, Pete caught up with Hix. "I still don't know much about it, except the action takes place on Mars."

"Well, basically the idea is we want to steal *Flash Gordon* without anybody in a position to sue us catching wise," Hix explained. "Oh, there's 3. Edward Bromberg going into Stage 3, Didn't know he was working here this week. Hiya, Ed, you look just terrific in that Viennese getup."

"Whoa now, Hix. We can't simply steal someone else's—"

"Eh? How's that again?" He cupped his hand to his ear. "You can stand here in the middle of the movie capital of the world and try to tell me nobody steals ideas. Anyhow, old buddy, with you to help out we'll stuff in lots of original crap."

"Okay, okay," said Pete. "Now I know June Maze is signed for our serial. But who's going to play Skyrocket?"

Six mean cowboys came bowlegging along the studio street.

Hix waved cordially at them. "The Dalton Gang. As to our serial epic, they've got Curly Horner for the lead. He's not bad for this kind of thing, so long as you remember to keep all his sentences down to no more than six words. Curly won a couple Olympic medals back in the early thirties."

"He was a runner."

"Whatever." They were strolling in the direction of a large salmon-pink warehouse. "Okay, so here's what Owls and I have worked out thus far in the idea department. Curly falls for June. Her old man is a rocket ship scientist with the California Institute of Rocketry, which, by the way, has to look a hell of a lot like Oxford since we have to use that standing set for it. Anyway, their romance barrels along at a terrific pace until the damn earth blows up. Wellsir, this prompts them to pile into her dad's experimental rocket. They figure to go to the moon. What with one thing and another, however, they miss the damn moon entirely and end up landing smack on Mars. Now the real fun begins, because Mars turns out to be a pretty wild and weird place."

"How exactly?"

"Ah, you've come to the heart of the matter, Pedro, my lad." Hix halted beneath an impressive palm tree. "I'll confide in you. I asked Owls to sign you on so that you might help answer this very question. You will be able, won't you, to cook up chapter after chapter of nice Martian stuff right away?"

"Sure," replied Pete. "I have lots of material left over from 'Warrior Queen of the Red Planet.'"

"Then we have not a problem in the world."

Pete shifted from foot to foot. "Listen, I'm not sure about the world-exploding business, Hix. Flash Gordon used that, Philip Wylie before him, even—"

"Can they copyright the world blowing up?" asked Hix. "And since a lot of people are afraid our old planet really is going to go blooey before the forties get much older, we need just such a snappy disaster to open our serial."

"How about a plague instead? Plagues are always good."

"Naw, not visual enough. A nice explosion is worth six or seven plagues any day."

"I still think . . . say, there's Tracy. Hey, Tracy!"

The slim girl had emerged from the big warehouse some fifty yards ahead. She wore tan slacks and a checked blouse; her auburn hair was braided. Turning now, she gave Pete a very brief nod and a very small smile before hurrying off in an opposite direction.

Pete started to take off after her, but Hix restrained him. "No time for romance," he reminded. "Our appointment with Owls is in less than ten minutes."

"She hardly paid me any attention at all." Pete was staring after the diminishing girl. "I mean, last night she—"

"Ah, there's one of the saddest lessons a young chap must learn. The difference between last night and this morning." Hix nodded at the nearby warehouse. "Another thing which is going to be sensational about *Skyrocket Steele* is the props. Owls has got a new special-effects man name of Dangler, and the guy is supposed to be a whiz. We're going to have rocket ships and ray guns and other weird devices that'll make Flash Gordon and Buck Rogers look like Our Gang playing games. Because of that Clifford Klaus dough in the background, there's a fat budget for us. So fat that most of the props are going to be life-size and not miniatures."

"They're working on the props already—before we even give them a scenario?"

"The basic junk, sure. It's being done mostly in this very warehouse." Hix approached the shut door of the big building. "I hear, too, Owls has got another big warehouse full of props out near our location setup near Palm Springs." Reaching out, he tried the doorknob. "Yow!"

"What is it?"

"Nothing, I guess. Got a funny twinge when I tried to open the door. Must have hit a nerve. Got to be careful with the magic Hix fingers." He took hold of the knob once more. "Wow. Happened again."

From around the corner of the building, trampling on flowers and fallen palm fronds, came a husky man. He was well over six feet high, dressed in a tan guard uniform. "Better go away, you guys," he advised.

"Don't know you," said Hix, scowling. "How come Skippy isn't on the door here?"

"His day off," said the big guard. "Nobody's allowed inside this one. Sorry. We don't want the other studios getting wind of what's being cooked up inside."

"Yeah, but I'm none other than Hix," he informed the guard. "This clean-cut youth at my side is Pete Tinsley. Together we are scripting *Skyrocket Steele*."

"That's nice, but we don't let anybody in."

"We ought to be able to see the damn props—they belong to our damn serial, after all," persisted the fuzzy-haired writer. "And I just saw Tracy Flinn come ambling out of this—"

"They don't like me to rough up any of the studio employees." The guard's beefy right hand dropped toward his holster. "But it—"

"We'll get permission from Owls," put in Pete. "C'mon, Hix, or we'll be late."

"Not even one quick peek?"

"Better hit the road, buddy."

Pete pulled Hix along with him. "Did you get the feeling there was something . . . some kind of force pushing us back, very unobtrusively, from that place?"

"Nope, but I got the feeling I'm going to yell my head off when we get to Owl's damn office."

"Wait until after I sign my contract," requested Pete."

4

"It's the standard Star-Spangled contract."

"That's what scares me."

Owls lifted off his spectacles and panted on them. "It's a better deal than he'd get at Republic or Columbia, Hix. Give it back." He held out a fat hairy hand.

Hix didn't return the contract. "Allow me to peruse it a bit more, Milt." He brought the many-paged document up closer to his squinting eyes.

Pete was sitting, uneasily, in a large tufted leather chair facing Owls's massive mahogany desk. Through the wide window behind the studio president you could see part of the forbidden prop warehouse, a stretch of thick African jungle, and the tip of Mount Vesuvius. "I read it pretty thoroughly myself," he said, uncapping his fountain pen. "Seems fair enough to—"

"Patience, Pedro." Hix carried the contract over to another of the large office's windows. "Let me scrutinize this in a strong light. Let's see . . . hereinafter known as the employee . . . lifetime of indentured servitude . . . chains to be removed only on the six hereinafter specified holidays . . . identifying Star-Spangled brand to be applied with hot iron to portion of said employee's anatomy hereinafter known as his backside . . . agreement void if employee attempts to escape over electrified walls . . . not responsible for damage done to said employee's backside (see Clause Twenty-six A for definition thereof) by the wild dogs let loose to—"

"What a wiseacre." Owls chuckled while he polished his lenses on his silk tie. "All kidding aside, Pete, this is a very fair contract. We guarantee you at least four weeks' work on *Skyrocket Steele,* at a hundred fifty per. With an option for your services on a weekly basis after that. Believe me—"

"Yeah, it appears to be relatively kosher." Hix, with an exaggerated bow and flourish, placed the document atop the desk in front of Pete and swiftly flipped to the last page. "You sign on that dotted line there, where it says Pathetic Serf's Signature."

"A wiseacre," repeated Owls as he readjusted his glasses. "We're expecting great things of you, Pete. I read a synopsis of your Red Queen yarn and it was damn good."

"The whole thing's only twenty thousand words. You ought—"

"Nix," said Hix. "A man in Milton's position can't waste the time it'd take to read through twenty-thousand words, many of them consisting of two or three syllables. Sign the contract like a good little chap."

Pete's pen dribbled blue ink on the contract. "Oops."

"Doesn't matter," Owls assured him.

He wrote his name on the indicated line, capped his pen, and pushed the contract across the immense desk toward the studio head. "Here."

Smiling, Owls dropped it into a drawer. "A pleasure to welcome you to Star-Spangled, young man," he said. "Especially if you can bail this schmuck Hix out of trouble."

"Who's in trouble? My basic concept is already terrific. What Pete'll provide—"

"Something wrong, Pete?" Owls inquired.

"Hm? Oh, no."

'You been twisting your head around. If you got a spine problem, let me recommend a Swede at the Beverly Hills Country—"

"I'm fine—must be a mild nervous twitch." Actually he'd been turning to gaze at the office door every time he heard something out in the reception room. He was hoping Tracy Flinn would come walking in. But she hadn't.

Owls checked his golden wristwatch. "I can spend six more minutes with you guys," he announced. "Suppose, Pete, you tell me what sort of stuff you're going to put in *Skyrocket Steele.*"

"Well," said Pete, turning away from the door. "You know about the explosion of Earth I guess."

"Sure, I ought to, since we're using old footage from *Phantom Invaders*. No, what I'm interested in is the Mars business. What happ—"

"Milt, we really don't want to take the bloom off this for you," put in Hix. "Why not wait until we lay the whole scenario, rife with thrills and chills, on you."

"So you couldn't give me maybe one small thrill now?"

"Listen, Milt, before we hand out any free thrills, I have a bone to pick with you." Hix eased up to the desk. "Why can't we take a gander at the props being built for our own damn serial?"

"Who told you you can't?"

"Some goon was on the brink of killing us in cold blood when we tried to sneak a look."

Owls detached his gold-rimmed spectacles again. "Well, Hix, as a matter of fact, we are keeping the *Skyrocket Steele* props under wraps for a while."

"I can see where maybe you want to keep rival studios from getting wind of what you're building, Milt. But I am a loyal true-blue—"

"We got to do it this way." Owls rolled his wrinkle-rimmed eyes ceilingward. "It ain't just my decision."

"What? You mean Clifford Klaus himself is—"

"I ain't saying. I ain't even admitting Klaus owns fifty-one percent of Star-Spangled. All I can tell you guys is—"

"You're gonna have to get rid of these bums."

When the office door bammed open, Pete shot to his feet.

It was only Thompson.

Clad in a check sport jacket and maroon slacks, the assistant producer came stomping over to Owls. "Hungry Holtzman is outside with ChiChi Cadela."

"So soon?"

"Claims he's got an urgent date over at MGM in forty-five minutes," explained Thompson.

"Bullshit."

"Sure, but you never can tell with Hungry. He's not like some agents—he occasionally tells you the truth."

Pete moved next to Hix. "Who's ChiChi Cadella?"

"Lad, don't you pore over the trades? She is known far and wide as the Bolivian Bombshell," Hix told him. "Noted for her enormous boobs and funny hats. Grapefruit here, bananas up here. With the European market shot to hell, everybody wants to make fillums that'll drive 'em nuts south of the border. Milt wants to sign ChiChi for a new musical extravaganza entitled *Honeymoon in Ecuador.*"

"What does she do?"

"Do? She has big tits. What more do you want?" Hix rubbed at his frizzled hair. "Oh, and I think she sings. In Spanish."

Owls was sighing deep chesty sighs. "That bastard Hungry knows I need this bimbo."

"Hungry has a knack for knowing what you need, yeah," said the bulky Thompson. "I don't think we better let him cool his heels while you waste time with Hix and his pet jerk."

"We resent that." Hix started for the door. "Sometime when you're less busy, Thomps, I'll return and poke you in the snoot."

"Ha," remarked Thompson. "And listen, Hix, when you cross the reception room don't stare at this babe's honkers. We want her to think SS is a refined joint."

"Can I pause to pluck a mango off her headgear? Or would—"

"G'wan, beat it."

"See you boys later. This is a crisis," said Owls. "I'll be on the lookout for that Mars stuff, Pete."

"It'll be worth the wait," Hix assured him, pulling Pete with him out into the immense white-and-gold reception room.

"They are," said Pete as they crossed the thick cream-color carpet.

Out on a palm-lined lane Hix said, "You mean you actually noticed ChiChi's frontage?"

"You'd have to go through contortions not to. Her bosom sort of dominated the place."

'Wait'll you see it in blazing Technicolor. Yeah, with Natalie Kalmus telling us how to shoot those boobs . . . but enough lustful thoughts for the nonce." Hix took hold of his friend's elbow. "Let me escort you to the Black Hole of Burbank, also doing business as the writers' building."

'I thought maybe Tracy would've dropped in while I—"

"Forget that lass. Sponge her from your mind," advised Hix. "From this moment on think only of eight-armed Martian warriors who—"

"Six," corrected Pete. "Martian warriors traditionally have six arms."

"Good, that'll be cheaper. Way things are going, they probably won't even let us see the Martians," he said. "Owls was pretty damn evasive about why the prop warehouse is taboo."

"Would Klaus really be involved in something like that?"

"I intend to dig further into the matter, my dear Watson."

At the end of a curving street stood a two-story stucco building, resembling something left over from a Southern California high school. A lone and forlorn sea gull was perched at the apex of the slanting red tile roof. Hanging from an open window on the second floor was a lacy brassiere.

"Whose office is that?" inquired Pete as they approached the building.

"That's just camouflage for Marzloff," said Hix. "He's really a homo."

"He's perverted, you mean?"

Hix grinned. "Being a pansy isn't exactly considered a perversion hereabouts, me boy," he said. "You won't have to worry about Marzloff making a pass at you—he's head over heels in love with Bronc Peeler.'"

"Bronc Peeler? You don't mean Bronc Peeler, the King of the Cowboys?"

"Actually the Queen of the Cowboys would be a better tag. Up these stairs and then take a right."

"You're not going to convince me Bronc Peeler is queer. I mean, back in East Moline almost every Saturday I used to see his movies when I was growing up. He rode a horse named Sniffles and, boy, when they tried to give him trouble, Bronc would fight and shoot and ride like nobody's business. Hell, I've based a lot of my pulp cowboys on him."

Hix bounded up the slightly sagging steps two at a time. "That's why they've dubbed Hollywood the city of illusions, Petrov," he said. "We can make queers look like tough guys, and vice versa."

Pete was sniffing. "What's that odor?"

"You'll grow accustomed to it. It's an amalgam of cigar smoke, booze, yesterday's sexual conquests, and Marzloffs cologne." He gestured with an out-flung arm. "We are now fast approaching the beautiful sector of the Black Hole inhabited by the fabled Hix, master wordsmith of Tinseltown. As our stomach sinks slowly in the west and our heart beats an anxious pit-a-pat, we draw nigh to its portals."

"Am I sharing the office with you?"

"Perish the thought, laddy buck. SS isn't that cheap. You have a dingy cubbyhole of your very own, right next to mine." He led Pete past his own office, which had *home of the brave* scrawled on the dusty frosted glass in lipstick, and tugged open the next door. "Don't go in for a few seconds. Give the rats a chance to clear out."

The room Pete saw on the other side of the threshold was about half the size of his living room. It contained a battered wooden desk, an ancient typewriter and a row of shelves along one plaster wall. "Not too bad," he observed. "Actually roomy compared to some of the spots I've worked in."

"One of the other assets," explained Hix, entering and crossing to the one window, "is a good view of the lot where some of the starlets play volleyball now and then. Ah, the sight of those jiggling boobs and those gnashing backsides is enough to make a strong man quake. Indeed, I've oft had to lash meself to my typewriter in order to bat out the brilliant copy they expect of me each and every day."

"Speaking of which, when do we start working on *Sky*?"

"A fitting question." Hix considered his wrist-watch. "It so happens I have an appointment for a sweaty carnal interlude at noon sharp, mere minutes from now. Yes, you can tell the hour is drawing near because already on my watch face Mickey Mouse has a hard-on. He knows full well—"

"You didn't tell me you had a date."

"Remind me to add you to the circulation list for my diary."

"What I mean is, Hix, Owls appeared eager for us to turn in some material. I'd like to earn that hundred fifty dollars for at least one week, so—"

"Relax. As Sam Jaffe told Ronald Colman in *Lost Horizon*, 'Don't get your balls in an uproar, my son.' " Hix scooted to the doorway. "We'll get right to work when I return at two. Make that three."

"Okay, I can start working on my own, I guess."

"Exactly. That's the old Star-Spangled spirit." Hix hesitated in the doorway. "Are you hungry? I can lead you to the commissary if you want. My only advice is, avoid the stew. They tave a habit of incorporating old props and—"

"Not actually hungry." Pete went over and sat behind the desk. The swivel chair squeeked. "Pretty comfortable."

"Wait till you've parked your carcass in it for several hours. Well, I'll see you again no later than three." Hix went dashing away down the corridor.

Pete swung around in his swivel chair to look out the window. No volleyball.

Getting up, he explored the bookcases to see what had been left behind. There was a neat pile of *Racing Forms* from 1940, a copy of *Kitty Foyle*, a *Film Daily Yearbook* for 1939, an empty gin bottle, the March 1935 issue of *Movieland* with Norma

Shearer simpering from the cover, a gray wool sock with the toes out, an ashtray shaped like a toilet, a blue-covered mimeographed script for a film titled *The Angel Strikes Back*, and numbers 3 through 6 of *Whiz Comics*.

Pete drifted to the window again. A shaggy gorilla was loping by, carrying a brown lunch bag.

"Are you allowed visitors?"

He spun, not sure what expression to attach to his face. "Sure you've got the right office?"

Smiling, Tracy tapped the white cardboard lunch box she had tucked under her arm. "Had lunch yet?"

"No, but I really ought to get settled in this—"

"I want to talk to you." The girl stepped into his office. "We could stroll somewhere and share our sandwiches. I've got a pastrami on rye and lox on a bagel. Any preference?"

"Impression I got when I was hollering your name like some rural bumpkin this morning was that you weren't much interested in having anything to do with me."

"My job here is such that I—"

"Hey, don't let me keep you from it then," he told her. "Or is this part of it? Make the green kid feel at home, don't take more than ten minutes."

"You really can be a nitwit at times." She put a hand on her hip, watched him with her head tilted slightly to one side. "I do want to talk to you, Pete, and this ramshackle building isn't exactly the ideal spot. Even if you're fasting, can we take a walk?"

She was as pretty as he'd remembered. Everything about her looked exactly right. "Okay," he said, "but could you make an effort not to be so damn enigmatic."

"I'll try," she promised.

5

The old dark house loomed up behind them, casting darkness down across the bright afternoon.

Tracy climbed the swayback steps, took a blue polka-dot bandana out of the pocket of her slacks, and brushed at the top-most step. "This spot okay?"

"Sure, it's sufficiently gloomy." He sat down beside her.

"They used this house in *Bride of the Monster* and *Dr. Gorilla's Secret.*"

"I've been thinking, Tracy, about what went on last night at the Zig Zag. Now—"

"Pastrami or lox?" She flipped the white carton open.

"Doesn't matter much. Last night when—"

"You must have a favorite between the two."

"Matter of fact, I've never eaten either a pastrami sandwich or a lox one."

"I thought all Hollywood writers spent a part of every day in a deli."

"I'm a Hollywood writer only in a geographic sense, so far. Mostly I eat at home—lots of fruit and vegetables."

"That must be good for you."

"It's cheap. Especially if you go to a market that specializes in wilted vegetables and overripe fruit at a discount," he said. "Once in a while, if I'm celebrating a magazine sale, I buy a stale cake at the day-old bakery."

She handed him a sandwich. "Try the pastrami."

"Thanks. But about last night."

"Pete, that's one of the things we have to talk about."

"You asked me to forget what went on, except I can't. How did you—"

"Want a pickle? That's practically a raw vegetable."

"No, thanks. How'd you make him jump?"

Tracy was looking into the white carton. "It's a knack I have."

"A knack? People don't have knacks like that, Tracy. In pulps maybe, but—"

"No one knows what I did except you."

"Dime Gallardo must have an inkling."

"He's too dim-witted. By now he's likely convinced you simply got in a lucky punch."

"Take more than luck to lift him to the ceiling." Pete gestured with his untasted sandwich. "That ceiling has to be ten feet up. You never so much as touched him, meaning you must—"

"If anyone finds out I helped you, I could be in. a real jam."

"Who? You're being cryptic again. Is Thompson making trouble for you?"

"No, Thompson is mostly bluff."

Pete put his hand on her arm. "Could be I can help you, if you're in some kind of trouble."

Tracy was looking not at him but at the standing set across the road. It was a Foreign Legion fort sitting on its own small patch of desert. The mild afternoon breeze fluttered the battle-scarred French tricolor on the lopsided pole.

"I'm not in any real trouble," the girl said. "If you drop this, things should be fine."

Pete stared across at the fort. "I remember seeing Ronald Colman in *Beau Geste* when I was a kid. The silent version. I kept after my mother until she promised me I could have a Viking's funeral when I died," he said. "Look, Tracy, I want to keep seeing you. Since we're both working at Star-Spangled, at the moment anyway, it ought to—"

"For a while, Pete, I don't think we better spend too much time together. Here or anywhere."

"But if—"

"Later on, when certain things get . . . worked out, we'll see."

"This conversation hasn't, you'll excuse my mentioning it, brought much clarity to the situation."

"Eat your sandwich."

He took a bite, chewed. "Is it someone here on the lot who's—"

"Bet you write dandy detective stories. You've a real gift for cross-examining."

"I think," he said, "I'll have the pickle after all."

"Here."

"Thanks."

"We will see each other sometimes after all," she said. "In the course of the workday that's inevitable."

"I'm only going to be working on this damn serial for four weeks. That's what the contract I just signed says."

"Oh, Hix'll stretch it to six at least."

"Even six weeks isn't exactly an eternity."

"Once you . . ." She suddenly dropped the white carton, doubled over, and made a moaning sound.

"Tracy?" He tossed his sandwich away, put an arm around her shaking shoulders.

She was breathing unevenly, mouth open. "Don't worry . . . I'm fine."

"You sure don't act fine. Is it food poisoning or what?"

The girl straightened. "I had a sudden sense of something evil and dangerous in the . . . What am I saying?" She shook her head, the braids flipping. "My mind must be wandering, Pete, I'm sorry. Only a little cramp, nothing serious."

"Wasn't it? The way you . . . Hold on!" He'd heard something behind him inside the gloomy Victorian mansion.

Letting go of Tracy, he got up and sprinted for the door. Yanking it open, he dived inside.

Darkness and dust surrounded him.

Then Pete saw a moving shadow—a thick shape that went darting across the immense hallway and into the living room on his left.

Pete followed, reaching the room in time to see the shadow shape go out a window.

"Pete, be careful in there," Tracy called from the porch.

He looked out the open window into the weedy alleyway. There was no sign of anyone. "I'm okay," he yelled.

Tracy, pale, was standing on the porch of the haunted house. "Was someone in there?"

"Didn't get a very good look at him. Husky guy, I'd guess," he said, watching her face. "You sensed that, didn't you? Before I heard the sound of his footstep, you knew someone was in there and probably eavesdropping on us."

"No, not really." She smiled a small smile. "I'm nothing more than an everyday secretary, Pete. You're imagining all sorts of abilities I simply don't have."

"Same way I imagined Dime flying around last night."

"Think I better get back to my office. I'm still a mite shaky."

Taking her hand, he helped her down the rickety wooden steps. "Any idea who that was?"

"Oh, most likely only a stagehand fooling around. They love practical jokes. Nothing to fret over," Tracy said. "Could have been nothing more than somebody sneaking a nap."

"It wasn't."

"You're not that familiar with the way things are inside a movie studio yet. Things we take for granted may seem odd or—"

"Yep, you're right. I'm a babe in the woods."

"I'm not trying to make fun of you."

He didn't respond.

When they were near the executive building, the girl gave his hand a brief squeeze and moved away from him. "Try to do what I asked," she said, smiling tentatively at him. "By the way, how was the pastrami sandwich?"

"Terrific," he replied.

6

Pete gave up trying to read *Kitty Foyle* and switched to *Whiz Comics*. "That's quite a knack Billy Batson has," he observed after a moment.

Hix came dodging into his office. "Sorry I'm late," said the frizzy-haired writer, catching his breath.

"Is it after three?"

"Don't you have a watch, Pietro?"

"Had a gold pocket watch my folks gave me when I graduated from high school," answered Pete, setting the comic book aside. "I pawned that last year when the Stimulating line changed editors and I didn't sell anything for seven weeks."

Hix smoothed various wrinkled spots on his clothing. "Never make love in a trailer, my son," he said. "Anyway, it's nigh on to four. Let us adjourn to my spacious office to labor over the Skyrocket saga."

"Interesting date?" He followed his friend into the hall.

"Insatiable is the word." Hix nudged open his office door. "Trouble is, this girl is definitely going to become a glittering star in the Hollywood firmament. Once that occurs she'll sure as shooting cast me aside like the proverbial . . . what is it people are always casting aside?"

"Old shoes."

"That's what Mona'll toss me aside like." He dropped into his cushioned swivel chair.

"Her name's Mona?"

"At the moment. Sit on that sofa. I smuggled it out of the prop department."

Pete eyed the ornate Victorian piece of furniture. "Impressive."

"Charles Laughton expired on that sofa in *Loves of Thackeray*."

"That accounts for the spots."

"No, the spots are Mona." He was frowning up at a blank patch on his picture-covered wall. "Son of a gun, somebody swiped my dart board again. Excuse me." Hix dashed out into the hall. He cupped his hands to his mouth. "We know who has Hix's dart board! The cops are closing in! You have exactly ten minutes to return it!" Back behind his desk, he said, "What have you concocted in the way of red planet excitement whilst I was at the front?"

Pete was studying the rows of glossy photos on the far wall. "You've added a few since the last time I was here. Is that Mona, the blond who signed her picture with a lipstick kiss?"

"Naw, that's Olga the toe dancer from Pasadena. Mona I'm not displaying." Hix knocked on his typewriter and rubbed his palms together. "I await your thoughts on the matter."

"Actually, Hix, I haven't done much in the way of work so far," Pete admitted as he tried out the prop sofa. "See, Tracy dropped by right after you left."

"Listen, we can't both spend our afternoons fooling around. We'll have to take turns or—"

"We just walked around the lot, talked."

Hix narrowed an eye. "Yeah? Well, you sure look like a guy suffering from postcoital depression," he said. "Are you absolutely certain you—"

"You know Tracy a lot better than I do."

"Not really. Her basic attitude toward me might charitably be described as disdainful."

"I can't quite figure her out."

"I'll give you a great insight into life, young man. You can boff 'em without understanding 'em at all. Strange as it seems."

Pete said, "Somebody was . . . spying on us while we were having lunch."

"Happens all the time around here. You sit in that commissary and some jealous scribe is all ears to—"

"We were over at that haunted house set. Some guy I didn't get a good look at was inside, listening."

Hix frowned. "Hollywood isn't only a tiny blotch on the map, it is also a state of mind which includes Burbank. Hollywood is the goofy capital of the world. So don't go letting a harmless peeping Tom worry you."

"This guy seemed to upset Tracy a hell of a lot."

"I would like to make a motion," said Hix. "Let us table any further discussion of our respective love lives, as colorful and entertaining as they may be, until after we get something on paper pertaining to good old Skyrocket Steele and his merry adventures on far-off Mars."

"You're right, I better start justifying my hundred fifty dollars a week." He took a pencil from his jacket pocket and borrowed the top legal pad off Hix's desk. "Okay, I'm ready."

"The events of the first chapter we pretty much have." Hix leaned back until his frizzled head touched a glossy photo of a girl in a Spanish dancer's costume. "By the way, when we get to the actual script the premier chapter has to run thirty minutes. Rest of 'em'll go twenty. It's traditional to make the first one longer, to establish things and lure the yokels into our web of breathless suspense."

"You sure we have the opening worked out? We're really going to go with the destruction of the world?"

"We is."

"What destroys the earth this time around?"

"Allow me to slip you another bit of advice, Pedro. Never ever let on that an idea isn't fresh and new. If Owls realized he could steal this stuff from the same places we do, we could be out on our ears," explained Hix. "I was inclining toward a giant meteor. That would tie in with the footage we have to incorporate. Or we could have the moon falling."

"The moon?"

"Yeah, that hasn't been done lately. How about this? We open on Curly and June in her dad's observatory. They're hugging, smooching a little. That way, see, we establish the romance angle *and* the scientific background. Okay, what do lovers need and dote on, in the movies anyway? Moonlight. So, being of a keen scientific bent, they're gazing at the moon through Pop's big telescope. All at once Curly stops fondling June and does a take. 'Holy shit! The moon's falling!' Not bad, huh?"

"I think a giant meteor's better," said Pete. "The moon falling is going to sound too impossible."

"Do my aging ears hear rightly? Is this the man who grinds out verbiage for such wild and woolly publications as *Stimulating Science*? Can he be chiding me over the improb—"

"Okay, the moon falls. What the hell."

Hix sat forward, grinning, hands flat on his desktop. "Right, Curly's an expert at this sort of thing. He's been a test pilot for her daddy's experimental rocket ships—hence his colorful nickname of Skyrocket. Juney asks, 'How long is it gonna take before that fucking moon hits us, Sky?' 'My calculations indicate about a week, honey.' 'Earth is doomed . . .'—Aha! There's the title for our first chapter. 'The Doom of Earth!' We need titles for all twelve of the buggers. Where was I?"

"Earth is doomed and . . ."

"She wails, 'We only have a week to live, dearest. So let's boff whilst we can.' Skyrocket says, a manly look on his puss, 'Not all of us will perish.' 'What do you mean?' 'Your old man and you and me can take his rocket ship and fly away.'"

"I thought they were going to fly to the moon. If it hits—"

"That was what I thought before I became divinely inspired. No, we'll have 'em trying to get to Venus, because the climate'll be good for the old guy's sinus trouble."

"Venus is all steam and heat. Anyone with sinus trouble would—"

"Okay, so the old fart's got an obsession with taking steam baths. They're never going to get to Venus, so it doesn't matter what it's like."

"There's another thing bothers me, Hix. How about the rest of the people on Earth? Skyrocket ought to be concerned."

"He's not Wendell Wilkie. He's going to save his own ass and his girlfriend's."

"The audience would think better of him if he had some humanitarian feeling. You know, he could say, 'If only there were some way we could help the rest of the world. Or at least our fellow Americans.'"

"And June says, 'You put a hundred and thirty million passengers in Poppa's rocket, buddy, and it ain't gonna fly for diddly shit!'"

"He sounds too selfish unless—"

"Wait, wait! I'm getting something great." Hix rubbed a hand over his fuzzy head, shut his eyes. "Yeah, the President of the U.S.A. calls June's pappy on the television phone. He tells the old gent to build as many rocket ships as needed to save America's population. 'We must mobilize to save our great nation, Professor Avon.'"

"That's the old guy's name?"

"Professor Avon, yeah. June's name is Lucille Avon."

"Lucille's a dumb name for a girl, but go on."

"The best pair of boobs I ever witnessed were attached to a lady named Lucille. Down in San Pedro one summer when I was fresh out of . . . Back to the scenario. The prez orders a thousand rocket ships. Prof Avon worries, 'I'll have to work my ass off to build that many in one week.' Ah, but he's gonna have an even bigger problem. His trusted lab assistant, Hans Van der Boom, is actually a Nazi spy. He doesn't want America to be saved, so he swipes the secret plans and sabotages the profs rocket factory. He even ties June, alias Lucille, to a generator or some factory thing and leaves her to die. Skyrocket gets wind of the fix she's in, saves her boody right out of the blazing factory. What a shot that'll make. We get a big sigh of relief from the yokels and then we hit 'em twixt the eyes with the next surprise. Just as Sky and Lucille are clinching and he's brushing the soot off her perky nose, he glances upward and does a take. 'Jesus H. Christ! My calculations must've been a little off. Here comes the moon now! It's gonna smack us in less than ten minutes.' We tag this chapter with the whole damn earth going boom. Is our hero in smithereens? Did he manage to cop one last feel before oblivion set in? Come back next week. In Chapter Two we show that seconds before the big explosion they scrambled into the profs one remaining rocket ship and took off." Hix stood up. "Sky comes across as a humanitarian, we got action, suspense, and romance plus one of the great cliff-hangers of cinema history."

"Sounds okay."

"Okay? It's brilliant."

"Thing is, when the moon starts falling, it's going to trigger a series of effects which—"

"Wait now, pardner," cut in Hix, holding up a hand. "Let me explain who we're aiming this extravaganza at. We don't want to woo an audience of be-whiskered lads from MIT and Cal Tech. No, we are after the millions of freckle-faced kids on the brink of puberty. They're riddled with acne and reek of sweat and bubble gum. They don't want scientific fact, they want action. And if June flashes a little tit, that's okay, too. Heroics is the main thing they crave—a lot of jumping around, fist fights, ray gun battles, rocket ships whizzing through space. They don't want scientific stuff about the boiling point of water and the density of lead."

"Looking at it from that point of view," said Pete, "what we have so far sounds perfect."

"You're damn right," agreed Hix.

7

The night Pacific was a wide ribbon of black along the horizon. Reflections of the scarlet candle holders seemed to flicker out in the darkness beyond the sparkling view window.

Boots McKay, giving a pleased shiver, said, "This is swell." She touched her cocktail glass to his. "Here's to continued success in the movie business."

Pete said, "Still find it hard to believe I've lasted an entire week out at Star-Spangled and collected my first paycheck today."

"It's amazing anyone could work six whole days with that sap Hix." The dark-haired dancer sipped at her Singapore Sling, then set the glass on the table and gazed casually around the crowded restaurant.

The Sea Shanty stood on a bluff in Malibu, two hundred feet above the beach. It was decorated with fishnets, polished glass floats, bright-painted anchors, life preservers, and several other nautical props that Pete, even though he'd sold five stories to *Stimulating Sea Tales*, couldn't quite identify. The restaurant was L-shaped, dimly lit, and the waiters, who all gave the impression they were aspiring leading men, wore nineteenth-century midshipman uniforms.

"Hix has been very helpful," said Pete.

"Because the jerk needs you," she said. "He's like that gunk that grows on the shady side of trees. A parasite. A lot of writers in this town get to the top by borrowing ideas from some poor dope."

"Hix has plenty of ideas of his own. He's got a good plot sense."

"He knows what plots to steal," she acknowledged, picking up her drink. "There is one thing about him I like. If he wasn't such a schmuck, he'd be interesting. He's cute."

"Hix? Is cute?"

Boots' nose wrinkled when she smiled. "I think so. But then I've always thought Mickey Rooney was a doll."

"They both have lots of energy."

Boots, frowning, studied him. "You'll excuse my mentioning it, but you look a little down in the dumps tonight," she said.

"We didn't, you know, have to celebrate your first successful week as a screenwriter at such an expensive joint. Four ninety-five apiece for a dinner borders on the outrageous. If you need it, I got five bucks in my stocking I can—"

"It's not that, Boots. I can afford the Sea Shanty."

"Well, I've been catching glimpses of you in the window, when you thought I was only mooning over the ocean view. You looked down in the mouth."

"Sorry. Doesn't have anything to do with you or my new job. Like another drink?"

"More than one, I get woozy," said Boots. "I didn't mention this before, so as not to detract from your celebration, but it looks like I'm going to get that part."

He smiled. "Hey, that's great. The one in the new Busby Berkeley movie?"

"Yes, it's called *Dancing Coeds*. They want me for the lead's kid sister. I can still pass for eighteen on the screen. Partly it's because I'm sort of flat chested."

"You're not exactly—"

"My legs compensate, though."

"Is it set for sure?"

"It's ninety percent certain. Which means it could still all go flooey."

"No, you'll land it for sure."

She held up crossed fingers. "I could use a break about now."

"If I can turn into a screenwriter overnight, then you ought to make it."

She glanced toward the bar across the restaurant. "My gosh, there's Monte Nightbridge himself."

Pete turned to look over his shoulder. "Where?"

"You missed him—he just fell off his stool."

"Oh, yeah, I see the headwaiter picking something up. That him?"

"Imagine that, Monte Nightbridge." She shook her head, awed. "One of the major stars of the silver screen in his day. He won an Academy Award in 1932 for *Captain Ahab's Revenge*. Gosh, back home in Detroit I used to cut his pictures out of all the movie magazines. Had a terrific crush on the guy."

"That was a few years ago. He hasn't done much but B movies lately."

"Booze," she said. "Hope he doesn't make any trouble for you."

"Me?"

"Monte Nightbridge's been signed for a part in *Skyrocket Steele*."

Pete blinked. "Which part?"

"The scientist."

"Professor Avon? We described him as 'a gentle, warm-hearted gentleman, burning with scientific dedication, a plump fatherly-type with iron-gray hair.'"

"Well, Monte Nightbridge's got gray hair."

Pete watched while they carried the fallen idol out of the place. "Guess I won't worry about casting."

Reaching across the small table, Boots put a hand over his. "You can tell me what's bothering you if you want," she invited. "Basically, Pete, we're pals, sort of a brother-and-sister act. It's some dame, isn't it?"

"In a way."

"So tell me about it already."

He shook his head. "Not ready to confide. See, the problem isn't exactly the usual romantic one."

"Boy meets girl, boy loses girl?"

"I met her, but there hasn't been any romance to speak of. She's fairly indifferent now, though the reason for that seems to . . . I'm puzzled as to what the hell is actually going on."

"She is cute," observed Boots. "In that unusual way—sort of foreign."

"Who?"

"It is Tracy Flinn you're avoiding mentioning, isn't it?"

"I keep forgetting you know more Hollywood gossip than Louella Parsons or Johnny Whistler. It's Tracy."

"She spends a lot of time with that Thompson bozo."

"He's one of her bosses."

"After-hours time."

"No, she's not involved with him that way."

"Believe what you want," said Boots, "but try not to get hurt."

"I can handle Thompson."

"Didn't mean that kind of hurt. This isn't the right kind of talk for a party." She picked up her glass. "Let's change the subject."

"Tell me more about your new part."

"I'll have over a hundred lines and three numbers," she said, "knock wood."

*   *   *

Pete carefully backed his '36 Plymouth coupe from between the big gleaming cars it was parked next to on the Sea Shanty parking lot. A gentle wind was blowing in across the night ocean.

He rolled his window down. "Who was that guy you were talking to while I got my hat?"

Boots replied, "Jon Hall. Didn't you recognize—"

"No, the little wispy fellow with the floorwalker's moustache."

"Oh, Franklin Pangborn."

"That's right. I've seen him a hundred times in pictures and never remember his name."

"He's sweet, though you can never trust a pansy."

"What? Franklin Pangborn's queer?"

"Sure, everybody knows that."

"Except me." He guided his car out onto the coast highway. "I ought to know stuff like that if I'm going to be in the business."

"If there's anybody you're not sure of, ask me."

"I even heard Bronc Peeler was."

"He is." Boots laughed. "So's his horse."

Pete was frowning at his rearview mirror. "This guy in the big black sedan's riding too damn close to our tail."

"Give it the gas."

"I am." They were speeding along a curving section of the night road that bordered a rocky hillside, which dropped down to the sea.

"Watch out!" Boots was twisted in her seat, staring out the back window.

The big sedan roared closer, then swung out beside Pete's old Plymouth. There was a huge gonging sound as the heavy car brushed his.

"Hey, jerk! Watch it!" Pete yelled out the open window.

45

He couldn't see who was in the other car. Three men in dark overcoats and pulled-down snap-brim hats.

The sedan nudged him again, harder.

"You're going to force us off the road, idiots!"

"Pete . . . I think that's what they want to do."

The sedan pushed at his car, sending it to the brink of the long drop down the cliff side. Pete fought his steering wheel and saved the Plymouth from careening off the road. "I better stop and—"

"You stop and I bet they'll shoot us!"

He tried to swing his car into theirs. That had no effect and once more the big sedan was shoving him toward the drop.

"Pete!" She clutched at his right arm with both her hands, eyes shut in fear.

All at once the sedan was gone from beside him. Pete had the crazy impression he saw it rise right off the road to go sailing up into the air. Clean over his wobbling Plymouth it flew, then went arcing away toward the dark Pacific.

Boots sighed out a breath and opened her eyes. "We're still alive," she said, surprised. "What the dickens happened?"

"We lost them somehow."

"You're right, I don't see their darn car anywhere," Boots said. She sank back against the seat, let her legs go wide. "We're sure lucky. Any idea why somebody would try that?"

"Not really, no."

Snapping her fingers, Boots sat up. "Dime Gallardo," she said with conviction. "You got into that brawl with the guy last week at the Zig Zag. Gallardo never forgets."

"It wasn't a brawl," Pete said. "I don't see why Dime Gallardo would try to kill us just because I threw a punch at him."

"Maybe they didn't want to kill us, only break our bones. Teach you a lesson," she suggested. "Jeez," how would I be in *Dancing Coeds* with my leg in a cast? That's a terrible thought."

"It won't happen again," he said quietly. "You're safe."

"Pete, don't try to do anything. Just lie low and leave these hoodlums—"

"I'll have to look Dime up and explain to him—"

"Don't! Keep clear of that guy," she said. "Hey, listen, maybe it wasn't them at all. It was more likely a drunk movie star. They're always doing things like this."

"I'll find out what happened," said Pete. "Then I'll do what has to be done."

8

The Sunday morning sun had only begun to warm the lower half of his bed when there was a tapping on the door.

"Are you decent?" Boots let herself in. She was dressed in white duck slacks, a fuzzy blue sweater, and a sailor hat. Under her arm was tucked a thick Sunday paper, its bright funnies glowing.

"You come over to read me the funny papers?"

"Better than that." Laughing, she plopped the hefty paper down near his covered feet, tugged out the first news section. "It's right here with all the junk about Hitler. 'Underworld Figure In Freak Accident. Alleged Hoodlum Takes Unexpected Dip In Ocean.'"

"Let me see." Pete took the first section of the *Los Angeles Times* from her.

"Don't you sleep in pajamas?"

"Bottoms only."

"So I won't have to turn my back when you get up."

He was scanning the story at the bottom of page one. "Cops found him and two others . . . fifteen feet out in the surf off the Malibu coast . . . no clear explanation of how they got there."

"Skip down to the good part."

"Gallardo's in the hospital with a broken leg . . . other two guys suffering fractured skulls." Pete lowered the paper. "Then they probably won't bother us for a while."

"If ever." Boots perched on the side of the Murphy bed. "But what do you think really happened?"

"Their sedan must've gone out of control, crashed down the hillside."

"Nope." She leaned, jabbed at a paragraph in the story. "Says right there there's no evidence the vehicle rolled down the hill. On top of which, Pete, there weren't any tire tracks on the sand."

"Could be the police didn't examine the site thoroughly enough."

"Those traffic guys are no dopes," she said. "Besides, they'd want to pin as many charges on Dime Gallardo as they could. If he smashed through a guardrail, they'd sure know it."

After drumming his fingers on the paper for a few seconds, Pete swung up out of bed. "Beats me then."

"That's a cute design on the bottoms. Is that geese?"

"Swallows. Going back to Capistrano." He edged into his tiny bathroom. "Excuse me while I shave."

Boots left the bed, which rose two and a half feet. "I had my peepers shut there when I thought we were going over the cliff." She dropped into the lone armchair. "Did you actually see those crooks go off the road."

"Not exactly." Pete worked up a lather on his shaving soap, dipped his bristly brush into it.

"It all seems very strange and peculiar to me."

He spread the warm foam over his face. "The paper calls it a freak accident, Boots. Let's settle for that."

"You're more muscular in back than I thought."

"I'm a regular Hunneker."

"Better—he's going to flab." Boots was leaning in the bathroom doorway, watching him shave. "Pete, I'm certain something weird happened last night. Don't you think it was maybe . . . you know, supernatural?"

"Nope," he lied, careful his eyes wouldn't meet hers in the mirror.

"Then what the heck made that car take a flying leap?"

"Maybe it didn't, Boots," he said. "It's possible those guys simply drove down to the beach on some little private road. The police didn't spot them until dawn, the whole incident could've happened a long time after they were chasing us."

"If they drove into the ocean, how come no tire marks in the sand?"

"Tide washed them away."

"Not according to the *Times*," she persisted. "And what broke Dime's leg? Joyriding along the beach wouldn't do that."

"Rival hoods could've worked him over with a baseball bat." Bending low over the cracked and stained porcelain sink, Pete washed his face. "We're speculating without enough facts. Wait until the papers give us more to go on."

Boots walked into the living room. "Hey, it's almost ten. Got to run," she said. "I'm going to a beach party with that guy who works for Busby Berkeley."

"Good luck."

"He's safe."

"With the part."

"I think that's ninety-five percent set now. Sweating out that last five percent, though is what's rough. See ya."

"Okay, bye."

There was no shower and he didn't feel up to getting into the claw-footed bathtub. After washing himself at the sink, he dressed in slacks and a sport shirt.

Six months ago he'd managed to finagle himself a set of all the phone directories for the Los Angeles area, through a girl who worked for the phone company. He consulted these now, kneeling by a sunlit window.

Tracy Flinn was listed in the third book he tried. The address was over in Sombra Canyon, on the other side of Beverly Hills. Pete stayed looking at the phone number for a long while. Then he copied her address on a corner of the *Times*.

"This calls for a face-to-face meeting," he decided, heading for the door.

The chimpanzee recognized him.

It was sitting in a red and yellow striped canvas chair on the small porch of Tracy Flinn's canyon cottage, very sedately eating Rice Krispies and sliced bananas out of a blue plastic bowl.

When Pete parked his coupe behind a long low sports car, Toko began making pleased chuckling noises and waving his spoon.

Pete surveyed the three other cars parked along the lane. "She's got company, huh?"

The chimp, carefully, plucked a dripping chunk of banana from his bowl and offered it to Pete.

He accepted, holding it gingerly in his palm. "Thanks."

The cottage was made of redwood and sat at the deadend of a narrow twisting lane. Stretching away from it was a wooded hillside topped by a grove of walnut trees. There were two other houses on the short block, larger than Tracy's and separated from her by wide sloping fields of high grass.

From inside the cottage came an assortment of sounds. A Benny Goodman quartet record was playing, people were chattering, a girl was giggling. Pete pushed the bell button.

The noise continued.

Toko made a loud appreciative slurp over his breakfast and then gave Pete an apologetic lips-back grin.

Pete knocked on the redwood door.

"Hey, it's the door," said someone inside.

"Maybe it's that half-wit apeman come to retrieve his chimp."

This last voice belonged to Thompson, and it was the burly Star-Spangled executive who yanked the door open to scowl out at Pete.

"Is this the Flinn residence?"

"You planning on mingling with your betters, wise-ass?"

"If there are any here," Pete answered. "Basically, though, I came to see Tracy."

"Uninvited. Not a good idea."

Pete took a step forward. "Nevertheless, I—"

"Pete, what is it?" Tracy appeared behind Thompson, wearing a pale green cotton dress.

"There's something I want to—"

"Suppose I toss him and the monkey into the lot over yonder?" suggested Thompson, starting to roll up a shirt-sleeve.

Tracy, reaching around the belligerent Thompson, caught Pete's hand. "I'm having a few people over for brunch. Come on in, won't you?"

Thompson didn't budge.

Using an elbow, Pete nudged into the cottage. "Pardon me."

"Jerk."

Tracy led him to the center of the living room, which was furnished with low and heavy mission-style wooden furniture. Bright serapes hung like tapestries on the white stucco walls, along with a large silver zodiac plate over the narrow stone fireplace. "I'll introduce you. This is Pete Tinsley, for those who don't already know him," she said. "Marzloff you probably already know . . . this is Bud Duttlinger, who's ramroding the stunts for *Skyrocket Steele* . . . maybe you saw the Lightbody Twins in one of their PRC musicals. This is Pattsy Lightbody and this is Bettsy Lightbody . . . No? Sorry, it's the other way around . . . and this is Dilly Dwiggin, the agent."

The immense dark woman in the double-breasted man's suit tapped ashes off her cigar, rumbled up out of her wood-and-leather chair. "Have you thought about midgets?"

"Not for the past few hours," admitted Pete.

"They're exactly what you need for this chapter play of yours. Tell Brocklehurst in casting I can get him a dozen, or two dozen if need be." Dilly put a hand on Pete's shoulder. "These are clean-cut, homespun midgets, too—not sex fiends like that Hermansdorfer troup. And what's Mars, after all, without midgets? I represent Major Wee and his Mighty Midgets, not one of them a smidgen over three feet high. Some considerably smaller. Picture this, Peter. The double moons of Mars rise over the red desert and there, facing Curly Horner, are twenty-four of the most ferocious midgets known to man, glaring at him. Screaming bloody murder and waving swords."

"Meaning no offense, Miss Dwiggins, but—"

"It's Mrs. Dwiggins. I have one of the few happy marriages in this crazy town."

"Meaning no offense, Mrs. Dwiggins, but midgets don't strike me as capable of being ferocious. What we have in mind is big husky fellows, with six arms."

"I don't have any six-armed actors in my stable at the moment, but I do have Vuko the Serbo-Croatian Giant. You've probably seen him wrestle."

Pete was anxious to follow Tracy, who'd gone into the kitchen. "No, I can't—"

"He's seven feet high from toe to topknot." The husky agent got a firmer grip on him. "The brow on the man is no higher than a gnat's fanny, and if you paint Vuko green you'll have half of America messing their pants."

"Why don't you suggest all this directly to Brocklehurst, since I—"

"Brocklehurst is being coy with me," admitted Dilly, puffing on her cigar. "Merely because my talent agency specializes in freaks, he's got the crazy notion I'm weird myself. Now, you can be in the poultry business and not have feathers, you can be a gardener and not lose your leaves in the fall. I can handle freaks and still be a simple Pasadena housewife. Have you thought of adding a pinhead to your script?"

"No." He tried to detach himself from her. "I can let you have Pinhead Malley, the nation's leading zip. He'd be perfect as the wicked king of Mars."

"We don't have a wicked king."

"How about an ugly president? I can get you Iron-jaw Milman."

"I'm not familiar with his work."

"He's the ugliest man alive," Dilly explained. "Due to a tragic bone disease in his youth, his face is a—"

"Excuse me, I think Tracy needs me to squeeze some more oranges." He wrenched free, started for the doorway Tracy had gone through so long ago.

"Hello, stranger," said the tall and handsome Marzloff, blocking his way.

"Hi, Marzloff. How's *The Three Saddlebums Ride Again* coming?"

Marzloff stroked his handsome forehead. "Absolutely awful," he answered. "That Simplicissimus is such a bitch. He knows not a thing about the real West. When I was over on the set he was actually insisting that Butch Mathis wear his chaps backward. Claimed that was actually the way the things ought to be worn. I told him, 'Listen, sweetheart, if there's one thing I know, it's how a cowboy dresses.' I really don't know why I allow myself to get involved in these technical things, since, after all, my primary job is to write. I shouldn't let some queen like Simplicissimus bother me at—"

"Him, too?"

"Beg pardon?"

"Tracy wants me in the kitchen. See you soon again."

"We ought to have lunch."

Pete sprinted by the platinum-haired Lightbody Twins, each of whom was startlingly lovely, and made his way into the small yellow kitchen.

Tracy was leaning back against the refrigerator. Thompson was close, towering over her.

"And I say we—"

"Hi, Pete. Can I get you something? The waffle iron's doing strange things, but I can offer you toast or—"

"Not too hungry, thanks. I'll fix myself a cup of coffee."

"Help yourself." Thompson stalked off into the living room.

"I don't seem to have won him over." Pete lifted the aluminum coffeepot off the stove, unhooked a mug from the rack over the sink, and poured.

"Thompson feels protective toward me," Tracy said. "He wouldn't actually hurt you . . . or fire you."

"Last night," said Pete. "I want to talk to you about what happened last night."

"Give me another clue." She made her eyes go wide. "Animal, vegetable, or mineral?"

"When you lifted Dime Gallardo's car off the coast highway in Malibu and tossed it in the surf," he said. "That's what I'm referring to."

Slowly she shook her head. "I thought you were a level-headed sort of fellow. Now, though, I'm starting to—"

"You have to be what happened." He eased closer to her. "I like your dress, by the way. Gives you an air of innocence."

"Thanks," she said, smiling faintly. "Pete, I honestly don't have the slightest idea what you're talking about. Did Dime try to do something to you?"

"He tried, I think, to kill me."

She took hold of his arm. "That's terrible. Maybe you ought to go to the police."

"How can I go to the cops. They'd ship me off to Napa or Camarillo," he told her. " 'Officer, this gangster tried to run me off the road, see, but then his car took off and flew into the ocean.' They'd call for the men in the white coats."

"You think I had something to do with Dime's accident?"

"Didn't you?"

"No. I read about it in the paper this morning. Never occurred to me it had anything to do with you."

"I'm not crazy—that much I'm sure of," he said. "Therefore, I know what I saw last night was no hallucination. I actually saw his damn black sedan leave the road and fly into the ocean. At the Zig Zag I saw Dime lifted off the floor and flown to the ceiling. Since you admit to having had a hand in that, Tracy— using this knack of yours—I think you were involved in what happened last night, too."

"We'd like another waffle."

"Come on in, Pattsy."

"I'm Bettsy."

"There aren't any waffles, but plenty of bread for toast."

The lovely platinum blond came into the kitchen. "Are you with Star-Spangled?" she asked Pete.

"Yeah, in the writing department."

"Oh, only a writer." Bettsy concentrated on popping two slices of bread into the silvery toaster.

Close to Pete's ear Tracy said, "Go away and come back around four. Everybody'll be gone. We can talk then."

"Do we have anything to talk about?"

Tracy hesitated. "Yes," she said finally.

9

Tracy upended a seashell ashtray over the wastebasket. "Did you get a chance to talk to Bud Duttlinger? He's really one of the top stuntmen in town— nearly as good as Dave Sharpe over at Republic."

"You ejected me before I could," Pete said. "I hardly got to talk to more than half of the Lightbody Twins."

It was almost four thirty, they were alone in the living room of the girl's cottage. There were still faint scents of burnt waffles, cigar smoke and heavy perfume in the air.

"I've decided," she said, sitting on the couch across from him, "I owe you an explanation."

"I think maybe you do, yeah."

Pressing her palms on her knees, Tracy said, "Do you have any brothers or sisters?"

"One of each. My brother Phil is a teacher in Des Moines, my sister is still in college," he replied. "But this is your explanation, not mine."

"Point is, I'm an only child," Tracy went on. "I was really a very plain and gawky kid—not that I've changed all that much. Confiding in anyone is very difficult. I haven't ever gotten into the habit."

"I'm not trying to grill you. I only want to know what's going on."

She took a careful deep breath. "Quite early I discovered I had this . . . knack," she said. "More than one really. I could sense things, get premonitions of what was going to happen. I also had the ability to move things."

"That's what they call a telekinetic ability."

Nodding, Tracy said, "Makes me sound odd enough to have Dilly Dwiggins for an agent, doesn't it?"

"When Dime Gallardo hit the ceiling, how exactly did you do it?"

"Simply by willing it," she answered. "I'm not, even after all these years of practicing it, all that certain how it works. I only know I concentrate on making a certain object move and it moves."

"This is like . . . something I write about for the pulps."

"Which is one reason I haven't wanted to talk about it."

"The business with the sedan last night . . ."

"All yesterday afternoon I had a terrible feeling something awful was going to happen to you," she said. "Telephoning you wouldn't have done much good, since I didn't have any specifics. You'd have thought me even wackier than you probably already do. Finally, when the premonition got really painful, I decided to drive over and keep a watch on you."

"You were by my apartment?"

She smiled. "I had to move my car twice because some midgets kept trying to pick me up. When you and your girl friend drove off, I followed to—"

"Boots isn't exactly my girl friend," Pete rushed in. "We're just friends."

"That's what people are always saying in the columns. The next thing you know they're in Reno tying the knot."

"You did the same thing to that heavy auto that you did to Dime himself?"

"When I saw him following you and realized what he was going to do, I grew darn angry." Her fists clenched. "I willed that car off the road and into the sea."

"Damn, if you hadn't, I—"

"I didn't want you to be hurt."

"You told me before something about getting in trouble if you confided in me," he said. "Are there other people involved in what—"

"No, nobody. What I meant was I didn't want anyone to know what I can do."

"Seems to me, with an ability like yours you ought—"

"To put on a mask and do good deeds? Like one of our serial heroes or some idiot in a funny book?"

"Not exactly, but—"

"I just want to pass for normal." She rested back on her couch.

Pete moved across, sat beside her. "You don't have to play guardian angel to me anymore," he said, taking her hand. "I'll be able to look out for myself."

"I shouldn't be as interested in you as I am. Somehow, though . . ."

He took hold of her, kissing her.

Tracy pressed into him, arms going around him, fingertips pressing into his back. "Would you care to stay to dinner?" she asked finally. "I can fix you most anything, except waffles."

*   *   *

Pete sat up suddenly in the unfamiliar bed. While he'd been dozing the day had died, everything was darkness outside and insect murmuring.

From the living room came a Morse code sort of beeping and a pale orange light.

Remembering where his clothes were scattered, he collected and got into them.

Tracy was sitting cross legged in front of the four-legged radio. Her auburn hair was down and she had a white terry cloth robe wrapped around her slim body.

The beeping had been coming out of the radio, the orange light from the parchment-shaded table lamp next to it.

Now the radio was saying, "Direct from Hollywood, the glamour capital of the world, here is Johnny Whistler and his Movieland Report. Brought to you each Sunday evening at this time over the Don Lee Mutual Network by Dr. HartwelFs Tooth Powder, for teeth that glow with good health, and Fast-Ex, the gentle though oh-so-effective natural laxative with the marvelous minty flavor. Now here's the most widely syndicated movie news columnist in America, gossip editor of *Movie Screen* magazine . . . Johnny Whistler."

"Hiya all from Hollywood, a town full of tinsel, romance, and heartbreak . . . Item . . . movie moguls are very unhappy about the way one of our town's leading swashbucklers keeps falling off the wagon. . . . Had lunch at one of Hollywood's posher eateries the other mealtime with lanky, laconic Gary Cooper. Coop swears his new pic, *Sergeant York*, will be one of the year's big box office smashes. . . . Don't know about that, Coop, since I personally believe a great many Americans don't want to think about war at all— even the so-called one to end all wars. . . . Lot of talk around that Humphrey 'Bad Boy' Bogart has finally landed a part he can sink his molars into. I've never liked Bogart's politics, but I have to admit the guy is a darn good actor. So I for one am anxiously awaiting for *The Maltese Falcon* to hit the silver screen. . . . Oh, how the mighty have fallen department . . . Once the idol of millions of frantic flappers, a screen idol who rivaled even the great Rudy Valentino, Niles Pomerene has just lost another job. The ex-millionaire, ex-heartthrob of the silent screen, was driving a bus that took tourists on a tour of the homes of the latest kings and queens of the movie capital. . . . And here's an open memo to my old pal, Milton Owls, hardworking head of Star-Spangled Studios. Dear Milt, you've earned an excellent reputation for fairness in this town. But unless you lend an ear to some of the working stiffs at your studio, you're headed for big labor troubles. Hate to see that happen to you, pal. . . . Let's hear about how you can have a smile as bright as that of any Hollywood star. Here's Jimmy Wallington. . . . And after that I'll be back to tell you what I think of Alice Faye . . ."

Tracy clicked the radio off. "Excuse my rudeness." She smiled up at Pete. "I always listen to Johnny Whistler every Sunday, no matter what. Him and 'One Man's Family.'"

"What'd he mean about trouble at the studio? Anything to do with *Skyrocket Steele?*"

"Oh, Roscoe Muldow's been making noises again. He heads up one of the guilds and they're miffed about a couple of things," she said. "No major problem at all. I'm a little surprised Johnny showcased it so."

Pete put a hand on her shoulder. "Do you—"

"I believe I vowed to fix dinner." She moved up and away from him. "Soon as I change."

"Sure, okay." He watched her cross into the bedroom and nearly shut the door.

He lowered himself to the spool-leg stool in front of the big cloth-faced radio. He switched the radio on, saw the light glow to life behind the station dial.

". . . here's what Linda Darnell has to say about her teeth . . ."

Pete turned to another station.

". . . means I ain't supposed to say dat?"

"No, I don't want to hear dat word."

"What word?"

"Dat word you just said what I don't like, Pick. An' iffen you says it again, I'se gwine to smack you one."

"Oh, I get you, Pat. If I says mud you is—"

Smack!

Pete tried another station.

"... pathetic parade of refugees fleeing the oncoming invaders. Helpless, forlorn, ragged. Women, children, old men. They trudge along, all they own on their thin backs or in the rude carts they pull along the clogged roadways. They seek only ..."

"Not cheerful enough." Pete switched the radio off.

There was a crash and a thud from the bedroom.

"Tracy?" He went running in there.

Wearing only a lacy slip, she was huddled beside the vanity table, a broken lotion bottle on the rug near her knees. "Someone's out there." She pointed at the window beyond the rumpled bed. "Something ... evil ..."

He knelt and put an arm around her bare shoulders. "You saw someone?"

"Sensed, really."

"Like at the studio that time?"

"Yes."

"Got a flashlight?"

"In the kitchen over the sink."

"Okay. Stick right here. I'll nose around outside."

"Pete, you'd better not. There's ... something very bad out there."

"Don't worry." He kissed her cheek, brushed at her soft silky hair.

He found the flash, clicked it on, and pushed out through the kitchen door. The darkness stretched away forever, deep and thick without a light or a star anywhere. Crickets clacked, night birds rustled in the brush. Far, far off, an airplane, its lights hidden in the overcast night, hummed across the sky.

Slowly, Pete swung the beam of the light in half circles. He edged around to the bedroom window.

"That you, Pete?"

"Yep, I'm investigating." The ground beneath the window was trampled. Someone had been here, watching.

He was able to follow the footprints away from Tracy's cottage for several yards. Then they were lost in a tangle of thorny weeds.

Pete made a complete circuit of the house, found nothing, and returned inside. Tracy was dressed in a skirt and blouse, sitting on the couch, hands clasped in her lap.

"Somebody was definitely out there," he told her. "A big guy, judging from his tracks. Have you had any trouble like this before?"

She shook her head. "No, and there haven't been any reports of prowlers or burglars hereabouts either."

"I'll call the police so—"

"No. I don't need them."

"Somebody's been lurking out there."

"Probably only a tramp. Lots of them around these days."

"You don't believe that, Tracy. You sensed real danger." He leaned, put his hands on her shoulders. "I'd better stay with you."

She looked into his face for several silent seconds. "Yes, I'd like that. Usually I love the quiet and solitude of this area, but tonight . . ." she said. "Pete, will you trust me?"

"About what?"

"I have to make a couple phone calls right away." she said, nodding at the phone on the end table. "Would you mind stepping into the kitchen and shutting the door?"

He shrugged. "Guess not."

"I like you."

"I figured as much." He went into the kitchen and shut himself in.

He heard her give the operator a number and then he caught the murmur of her conversation. No words, though—not a hint of whom she was talking to.

He paced the linoleum floor for a spell. Noticing the waffle iron, he said, "Might as well see if I can fix it."

10

Pete stopped whistling.

He braked his coupe, leaned his head out the window to get a better look at what was going on around the gates of the Star-Spangled Studios this foggy Monday morning.

Roughly twenty men were surrounding a green Chewy that was stopped ten feet onto the studio grounds. Shouting, waving fists, they closed in on the car to commence rocking it.

"Scab!"

"Fink!"

"Fellas, fellas!" pleaded old Billy the guard. "Let Mr. Dangler on through. You're blocking the way for a lot of other folks."

"Dis guy's a rat!" bellowed a stocky, curly-haired man of forty. He was clad in a gray work shirt and whipcord pants. There was a large union button pinned on the visor on his floppy gray cap. "He's takin' da bread outa our mouths!"

"Scrab!"

"Goon!"

"Union buster!"

The green Chevrolet was being bounced wildly from side to side. The lean bald man inside was smacking into the ceiling and the shut windows.

"I don't want to shoot none of you!" Billy drew his pistol and waved it in the air.

"Who's side ya on?" demanded the familiar-looking man in the gray cap. "Are ya wit da bosses or us wage slaves?"

"C'mon, Roscoe, you know I'm—"

"Fink!"

"Scab!"

"Goon!"

Pete shifted into low gear, started his Plymouth ahead. There was a patch to the left of the labor dispute he might be able to squeeze through. Watching for his chance, he rolled forward and made it onto the lot.

"Good morning, Mr. Tinsley," called Billy. "Excuse the riot."

"Think nothing of it." He drove over to the writers' lot and parked.

Wally Reisberson, an incredibly tanned and handsome man in a camel's-hair polo coat, was leaning against his Cord deep in conversation, with a beautiful red-haired actress. He toyed with her hair with a gloved left hand while they carried on their murmured talk.

"Morning, colleague," said Pete as he climbed from his old car.

"Who's that?" the beautiful redhead inquired as Pete walked away.

"Nobody," said Reisberson.

"Fifty thousand dollars a year, huh?" Pete said to himself. "Well, I'll make that someday, too."

There were two brassieres hanging out of Marzloff s window this morning. Maybe it was a signal.

Hix, in an impressive Hawaiian shirt and white slacks, was already at his desk, feet up and tossing darts at his board. "Top of the morning, Peter," he said.

Pete ambled in, sat on the Victorian sofa. "What's all the business at the gate?"

"What's happened to you?" Hix gestured with a dart. "You look like the cat who slept with the canary."

"Nothing."

"You won't get away with that kind of alibi, lad. Grogan, fetch the rubber hose," said Hix. "It can't be Boots—she wouldn't produce such a glow. You're face is lit up by what we call, technically, an SEG. Therefore, I conclude the lady in the case is none other than Tracy Flinn. Come clean."

"I did see her yesterday."

"Mingling with the ruling class can be bad for us peasant lads."

"I like her."

"So I've heard."

"Johnny Whistler was predicting labor trouble here," he said. "Is that what's going on?"

"You mean the uprising?" Hix massaged his frizzy hair. "Yes, that's Roscoe Muldow who's leading the gang. He's president of the Prop Makers Local."

"They were trying to tip over Dangler's car. He's the one who's doing the special effects for *Skyrocket*, isn't he?"

Hix nodded. "Owls made some kind of deal with the IA union, which Muldow's people don't belong to, allowing Dangler to work on the special props. Roscoe wants his boys to make all the props—he's down on Dangler and his corps of special technicians."

"What's the IA?"

"International Alliance of Theatrical Stage Employees & Moving Picture Machine Operators, and don't ask me how they got involved with the making of props and special effects."

"Will all this foul up our serial?"

"Naw. Owls will offer Roscoe another two bits an hour and it'll be settled."

"We still haven't even had a look at the props."

"Remind me to throw one of my famous tantrums next time we're in the vicinity of Milt," said Hix. "All we've laid eyes on thus far are Dangler's sketches."

Pete rubbed at his chin. "That Roscoe guy looks familiar."

"Lionel Stander," said Hix.

"Huh?"

"He's almost a dead ringer for Stander, the noted tough-guy character actor."

"Right, he is," said Pete. "Except that's not what I was thinking of. Got the feeling I've seen him somewhere else."

Hix raised both hands high, spun in his swivel chair and salaamed toward the window. "Oh, Allah, send us inspiration so we may bat out many glorious pages of crap this day," he said. "Shall we begin? But wait, there's a memo here someplace from the head office." He slapped at the desktop with both palms. "Let's see . . . mash note from Connie Bennett . . . fan letter, gushing over my prose style, from John Steinbeck . . . unpaid bill for intimate surgery from a noted Mexican sawbones . , . Aha! Here it is, Inspector Blake— a memo from Milton X. Owls. I long thought the X stood for Xavier, as in Cugat. Doesn't stand for anything. It's just there to keep the Milton from bumping into the Owls. Ahum. 'Boys, it's great!' Meaning the scenario we turned in last Friday. 'I love it. You guys are great—another Hecht and MacArthur. Don't ask for a raise. Attached find list of minor changes to be made.' There follows a document which rivals the Constitution and the first six chapters of *War and Peace* in length and sweep."

"So he didn't actually like it?"

"No, no, Milt loves the basic scenario," Hix assured him, dropping the multipage memo onto the other paper debris on his desk. "The changes mostly amount to adding more space-ships and ray guns. And we can't have tails on the wolfmen of Mars."

"How come?"

"Too expensive."

"But no big changes in the plot or the scenes?"

"Hardly a one," said Hix, grinning. "I must tell you, Petrov, we make a great team. Usually I have to do a couple or three re-writes on a scenario before I can get started on the script. When I penned *The Phantom Vigilante Rides* I had to produce no less than five for Milton."

"We're ready, then, to start the actual script?"

"Exactly,—and with some haste, since Milt wants to see several chapters almost immediately," said Hix. "Have you been studying those old scripts of mine I donated to your education?"

"Sure, nights at home."

"Except for last night," said Hix. "Wow, Love Finds Andy Hardy. I feel responsible in a way, since I did bring you and the enigmatic Miss Flinn together."

Pete stood up. "Do you know if anyone around the studio has been bothering Tracy?"

"A goodly portion of the male inmates have a yen for the lass. Though I've never heard tell of any nastiness. Why?"

"Last night—"

The phone in the next room rang. That was Pete's office.

He ducked out, ran over to answer it.

"Hello."

"Wanted you to know I arrived safely," said Tracy.

"You could have come in with me in my car."

"That wouldn't have been exactly discreet, as I already mentioned."

"Still, I—"

"Pete, I won't be able to see you tonight after all. Something's come up."

"Trouble?"

"Business."

"We can have lunch instead of—"

"Not today. Today I'm going to be all tangled up with the affairs of Star-Spangled," she told him. "Let's try for tomorrow."

"Long way off."

"I know . . . well, I have to go. Bye."

"Sure, goodbye." He stood there with the receiver in his hand for nearly a minute.

When the switchboard girl asked, "Number please?" he hung up.

11

SCENE 52. Interior. Rocket ship.

PROFESSOR AVON is looking at the controls, concern clearly showing on his face. SKYROCKET notes this and leaves his seat next to LUCILLE to move swiftly to the old scientist's side.

SKYROCKET

What is it, Prof?

AVON

Good heavens, we . . . um, oh, nothing at all, Skyrocket.

SKYROCKET

You'd better level with me. I think something's wrong!

AVON

(lowers voice) Very well, Skyrocket, I'll confide my suspicions to you. But we don't want to upset Lucille.

SKYROCKET

You can trust me on that score, sir.

AVON

Take a look at the Vizascope.

SKYROCKET

Good gosh!

AVON

Exactly, my boy. The planet we're fast approaching is not Venus!

SKYROCKET

No. I can see canals, red desert. But it can't be! Are we going to land on Mars?

AVON

I'm very much afraid that we are!

*   *   *

"Not bad," commented Hix, reading over Pete's shoulder as he typed. "Chapter Two bids fair to being even more socko than One."

Lifting his fingers off the keys, Pete said, "I'm not exactly keen on the title for this chapter, though."

"'Terror on Mars!' is an absolutely splendid title. If they gave Oscars for the second chapters of serials, we'd be a cinch to cop one." Hix strolled to the window of his partner's office. "Terror happens to be one of my favorite words, and a lucky one. I make it a point to use it in all my serials at least once. In *The Phantom Vigilante Rides Again* we had 'Terror in Texas' and in *The Great Air Mystery* there was 'Terror from the Sky!' We had a nifty scene in that one, wherein the heroine has to parachute out of the burning airliner in her nightie. Had 'em jacking off in movie palaces from coast to coast."

"One of the reasons for my lack of enthusiasm is because the word's been overused."

"You can't overwork a magnificent word such as *terror*," insisted Hix. "You're probably being over-critical because your love life has done gone sour."

"I still can't figure her out." Pete pushed back from his desk. "Sunday we were great friends. Here it is Thursday and I've barely seen her all week. She keeps dodging me."

"Poor peasant lad, it's your sad fate to have fallen in love with a princess."

"Still could be she and Thompson are—"

"Come, come, old thing. She's enigmatic, not stark raving goofy."

"Are they playing volleyball out there?"

Hix was gazing out the window. "Game called on account of rain," he said. "Speaking of giving way to madness, Pedro, I have done a foolish thing myself."

"You're not going to marry Mona!"

"Mona and I are no longer an item. She's begun, as I prophesied, her climb up the ladder of success. The latest rung brought her into the bunk of an assistant director over at Paramount."

"What area of foolishness are you going into?"

"I telephoned Boots McKay and invited the wench to dine with me this very night."

"You hate her."

"The other evening I found myself in a grind house in Santa Monica. The double bill consisted of *Bulldog Drummond at the Circus* and *Hot Tamales in Paris*," explained Hix. "When our Boots appeared, wrapped all in gauze for the Love Clinic Number, a strange feeling stole over me. At first I thought my fountain pen was leaking, but I soon realized it was something more than that. I was reacting to the girl's attractiveness."

"I imagine she turned you down."

"There's the curious thing,—she didn't. Thus I have to zip away from here soon to don my evening attire."

"She did mention once she thought you were cute, reminded her of Mickey Rooney."

"Rooney? That shrimp? I tower over him a good two inches."

"She thinks he has sex appeal."

Hex left the window, grinning. "You can knock off for the day."

"Nope. I want to finish this scene."

Hix halted in the doorway. "Save the first encounter with the six-armed green warriors for me."

"It's yours," promised Pete. "Give my regards to Boots."

"Give my regards to Boots," sang Hix, shuffling off along the hall. "Tell her, 'Hello, Toots.' Ask her questions that are moot . . ."

* * *

SKYROCKET

Mars! This is quite a surprise, Prof!

AVON

Worse than that, Skyrocket. Look into the Vizascope while I focus on the desert area where we must land. Here, I'll adjust the Enlargograph.

SKYROCKET

Good gravy! Green men!

AVON

Six-armed green men. Giants by the look of them.

SKYROCKET

Yes, and in each of their six hands a wicked-looking sword. I think, Prof, we're going to have a fight on our hands!

12

He saw five Foreign Legionnaires disappear into the thickening mist. Pete turned up the collar of his sport coat, tugged down the brim of his hat. As he was about to cross the street leading to the parking lot, he heard a low hissing.

A gleaming silver Rolls Royce came rolling out of the mist, tires whispering on the damp roadway.

In the back seat was Clifford Klaus, the multimillionaire who was supposed to own half the studio.

"Sure, it's him. He looks exactly like the photo that was in *Life* last week." Pete slowed, watching the retreating car over his shoulder.

It was driving in the direction of the forbidden prop warehouse when it was swallowed by the heavy fog.

While Pete, stopped still now, was watching the spot where the car had been, he saw Tracy.

She materialized out of the grayness, went hurrying across the street some hundred feet from him, and disappeared again.

"Tracy!" He started after her.

Light showed at the thick frosted windows of the warehouse. Klaus's automobile, empty, stood by a side entrance.

"Bet she's in there, too."

Hearing the noise of someone approaching, he ducked behind a palm tree.

The guard trudged by in his circuit of the building.

When the guard was lost in the mist, Pete dashed up to the building. He pulled himself up by the sill until he was on eye level with the window.

He couldn't see anything—the frosting prevented that.

All at once the window came swinging out. Pete let go, falling back into a decorative hedge.

A backside—a vaguely familiar one—appeared in the opening. Then Roscoe Muldow of the Prop Makers Local dropped to the ground and let the window swing shut.

Grunting, he swung around and saw Pete. "What da heck you doin' here, kid?"

"Hello, Roscoe." He was free and clear of the brush. "You know my dad is a member of the AF of L and I'm all for solidarity. Can you tell me what's going on inside this place?"

"A union supporter, huh?" Muldow tugged off his cap. "Den youse'll get a kick outa takin' a squint at me union button."

"Attractive, but actually I'm more—"

"Naw, give it a real once over," urged the union leader. "Notice how da ting moves back an' fort' in me mitt. Tick tock, tick tock, like one of dem pendulouses. Makes ya sleepy, don't it? Sleepy, sleepy, sleepy. . . ."

*   *   *

LUCILLE

You're keeping something from me. What is it?

AVON

Nothing to worry your pretty little head over, my dear.

LUCILLE

Sky, we're in danger! I know it!

SKYROCKET

We may get a rougher reception than we bargained for, darling. But don't worry. . . .

*   *   *

Pete shook his head. He pressed his fingertips to the spot between his eyebrows.

The old alarm clock on his office bookshelf showed it was after seven in the evening.

"Last time I checked I swear it was about five thirty." Leaving his typewriter, he went over to shake the clock. "Did I doze off at the machine?"

He rolled the latest page of script out of the typewriter, added it to the pile on the left side of his desk.

When he took his coat from the prop brass pole hanger in the corner, it felt damp. So did his hat.

"How the hell'd that happen? I haven't been out of here since noon and there wasn't any rain then."

Coat and hat on, he sat again in his chair. "Yeah, and I . . . I have the impression I saw Tracy, just awhile ago."

Impossible, though. He'd been right here working on *Sky-*

rocket Steele ever since Hix left. He couldn't have seen the girl or gotten wet.

"I've only been a screenwriter for two weeks. I shouldn't be having a mental crack-up so soon."

His phone rang.

Pete grabbed up the receiver. "Hello."

"Is that you?"

"No, I don't think so."

"Hix, cut out the trick voices," said the girl on the other end of the line.

"I'm not Hix."

"This is Mona and you better not try to kid me, Hix."

"Mona, this is Pete Tinsley. Perhaps you've heard Hix speak of me, his partner," Pete explained into the phone. "You've got the wrong office. Even if you didn't, Hix isn't in."

"Yeah, then where is that so-and-so?"

"Gone for the day."

"Tell him," said Mona evenly, "he better call me tonight."

"I'll, should I by any chance encounter him, convey the message."

"Shit, you talk just like he does." Mona hung up.

Pete went home.

13

"What's unique about this restaurant is, it isn't shaped like anything. Not shaped like a derby, a milk bottle, an orange."

"How's the food?"

"Better than in our commissary," assured Hix. "Meaning it borders on the edible."

It was a mild Friday afternoon. The two writers were walking along one of the Burbank streets near the studio.

Hix, stuffing his hands in the pockets of his cocoa slacks, bounded a few steps ahead, leaped and clicked his heels together.

"You seem in a jolly mood," remarked Pete.

"In contrast with your dour person John Brown's body would look like a bucket full of sunshine," said Hix.

"I've got things on my mind."

"Why don't you try to forget Tracy until we—"

"Besides Tracy."

Hix halted in front of a narrow cafe with the words *Pearl's Place* in gilt on its sparkling front window. "We have arrived," he announced. "There is no Pearl, by the way, so no need to send her your best after the meal. Joint's run by a pair of old queens who are terrific cooks."

Pete hesitated. "This is a queer joint?"

"Would I drag you into a den of perversion and sin? Pearl's is owned and operated by practicing sissies, but it opens its portals to gourmets of all persuasions." He pushed through the swinging doors.

Pete followed.

The interior was small. The tiny round tables were crowded close; each had a checkered tablecloth and a single yellow rose in a thin glass vase. The walls were covered with a strawberry-pattern paper; each window was half-masked with a crimson café curtain on a brass rod.

"Hi, Franklin! You're looking very dapper."

"Is that Franklin Pangborn?" asked Pete in a low voice as they were led to a far table by a matronly waitress.

"The same. Thanks, Martha."

"A pleasure, Mr. Hix."

"This is my friend and colleague, the renowned Pete Tinsley."

Martha's plump face brightened. "I believe I read a yarn of yours in *Stimulating Sea* only last month. Although it was by-lined Captain Peter Tinsley. Would that be you?

"Yeah, they tack those ranks on in that particular mag," he said. "Actually I'm not a Navy man."

"I enjoyed the story none the less." She left them with the day's menus.

"Gad, your public is everywhere." Hix turned, waved at someone at a distant table. "Good to see you, Bronc. Is your horse getting over his influenza? Good."

"Is that Bronc Peeler?"

"Don't you recognize your boyhood idol?"

"He looks different without his Stetson," said Pete. "Listen, Hix, are you sure this isn't a homo hangout?"

"With the exception of Franklin and Bronc, everybody else is okay," Hix said. "Now suppose you tell me the latest cause of your gloom? Can't be our script, because that's dynamite."

"Last night I worked late."

"A filthy habit. It'll make hair grow on your palms."

"I think I lost an hour."

"Once in Tijuana I lost three days."

Pete said, "This wasn't because of drink or anything. I have the feeling I blacked out for fifty or sixty minutes. I may even have gone out somewhere and wandered around."

"Could be sleepwalking. Did you ever do that before?"

"No, I've never been a somnambulist."

"Well, let's see if we—"

"Heil Hitler!"

"Long live the Fuehrer!"

Shouting had grown up outside the restaurant, along with the sound of clomping horses.

"What the hell's that?" Pete stood up.

He and Hix dodged their way among the tables to the front window.

Parading by on the street outside were uniformed men on prancing horses. The uniforms consisted of tan jodhpurs, highly polished black boots, and silver shirts. Leading the pack was Fritz Henzler.

"Aw, it's only Henzler and his German-American Horse-man League," said Hix. "I thought maybe we'd been invaded by Nazis and I could take the rest of the day off."

The horseman behind Henzler was carrying a Nazi flag.

"They're allowed to do that?" said Pete, watching the silver-shirts go riding by. "Wave swastikas around and all?"

"This is a democracy," Hix pointed out. "You can do all sorts of idiotic things in a democracy, provided you have the proper permits. Henzler and his bully boys stage these little parades periodically. He knows this area has a high Jewish population."

"Ach!" cried one of the silver-shirts, toppling from his horse into the afternoon street.

"This is the part of these demonstrations I most enjoy," said Hix, massaging his frizzy hair. "When the peasants start tossing bricks and assorted dornicks."

Pete returned to their table and picked up the mimeo-graphed menu.

"Three Nazis knocked off their horsies in less than a block," said Hix, sitting opposite. "That appeals to the rowdy in me."

"I've got the feeling we'll be in uniforms ourselves pretty soon."

"I'd look absolutely great in that tan-and-silver ensemble. It brings out the Mickey Rooney in me."

"How was your evening on the town with Boots?"

"Terrific." Hix grinned. "The lass is a good deal less dopey than I originally surmised."

"Doesn't have a brain the size of a pea?"

"On the contrary, she's quite bright," said Hix.

Pete dropped his menu on the checked cloth. "I feel almost like a matchmaker."

"But enough of the adventures of Don Juan," said Hix. "Let's get back to this problem of yours."

"If anything more strange happens, I'll see somebody."

"A doctor?"

"First I'll see Tracy," Pete said.

Pete worked late again.

The venerable alarm clock had wound down at ten P.M. Pete kept typing, not bothering to rewind it.

There was nothing but dark and silence outside.

Most studio activity had long since wound down, too.

*   *   *

SCENE 63. Exterior. Martian desert.

SKYROCKET, the PROFESSOR, and LUCILLE stand with backs pressed against their rocket ship hull. There is fright written on the girl's pretty face, her bosom heaves. AVON seems bemused. SKYROCKET faces the charge of the green warriors with a smile of grim determination. He holds his ray gun at the ready.

LUCILLE

They're going to kill us!

SKYROCKET

Not without a fight!

*   *   *

"Plenty for today." Pete stretched his arms high, yawning. He added the newest page to the pile. "I haven't blacked out or anything."

Turning off his desk lamp, he left his office. There was only a pale night light in the hallway.

No stars tonight—nothing but gray overcast filling the sky.

He yawned again, hunched his tired shoulders. The parking lot seemed a long way off.

Right after he'd passed the prop warehouse he heard foot steps.

Running steps behind him.

Stopping, he glanced back.

There was a man hurrying toward him through the night. A man in his early thirties, his face touched with fear. His mouth was open wide, he was running hard.

A silver-shirt, realized Pete as he stepped back against a palm tree.

The running man wore the uniform of the German-American Horseman League.

He didn't notice Pete at all, kept on going, gasping for air, stumbling some.

There was no noise, but something made him look up.

"Holy Christ!"

77

It was a rocket ship, drifting across the dark at an altitude of not more than a hundred feet.

14

The silver-shirt was running for the studio wall.

He never reached it.

A panel in the silver belly of the hovering ship slid silently open. The barrel of a strange chrome gun came protruding out. There was an odd humming; a beam of sizzling white light came shooting down.

When the beam hit the runner in the middle of his back, his arms and legs went wide. He looked, for a few seconds, like a jumping jack that's had its string yanked. Then he collapsed into a hedge.

"Those are props," murmured Pete. "They're not supposed to work."

The ship was immense—the size of an airliner at least. It was one of the serial sketches come to life, except there was something . . . unearthly about it. The silence was unsettling, too. The rocket ship wasn't roaring the way they were supposed to; it came floating through the overcast night in some manner Pete couldn't understand.

Forcing himself to stop gawking up at it, he went trotting to the fallen intruder.

"Wonder if the guy's dead."

No—he was breathing.

As Pete was bending to touch the unconscious man, he heard a rustling to his left.

Someone was approaching him. A tall man in coveralls and a wide-brim hat. In his gloved hand he held a prop ray gun.

Straightening up, Pete said, "You're Dangler, aren't you?"

The man halted ten feet from him. The ray gun swung up to aim straight at him.

"Hey, whoa," Pete told him, "I'm on your si—"

The beam of crackling light leaped from the gun barrel to his chest. He felt as though an enormous wave had struck him, knocking the breath out of him. Needles seemed to be sprouting all over his nervous system—it was like bumping a hundred crazy-bones at once.

He tried to breath, struggled to grab hold of something that would keep him from falling.

No good. He fell to the grass.

*　　*　　*

". . . weren't supposed to hurt you. Darn it, Pete, you've really got to stop walking into things."

He was sprawled on something moderately familiar.

"They thought everyone was gone. You . . ."

Lost it.

The room came back after a moment. This was Tracy's cottage—he was laid out on her bed. The auburn-haired girl was sitting on the edge, bending over him.

"What the . . . the hell . . ." His voice was high-pitched and sputtery—something that might come out of a cartoon cat. Nevertheless, he made another attempt to speak. "What . . . did they . . . do to me . . ."

"You'll be fine in another hour or so," she assured him, pressing a warm hand to his forehead. "At least, all our field tests indicate that."

"You using me . . . for . . . for a damn . . . guinea pig?"

"Nothing like that," she said. "Dangler got rattled, thought you were another of those damn Nazis, that's all."

"That's all?" He attempted to sit up, discovered he couldn't. "You people treat me . . . like . . . some green Martian out of . . . *Skyrocket Steele*. Listen . . . those are props . . . they—"

"Relax. Rest a little longer."

He shook his head, causing Tracy to go spinning away from him. "My life . . . since I met you . . . it's turning into . . . into a pulp novel," he said. "What time is it?"

'Must be around four in the morning."

'I was out cold for . . . five hours?"

"The usual period is six to eight. Since you're in fairly good shape—"

"What kind of conversation is this? Here . . . we're sitting here . . . collapsing here in my case . . . talking matter-of-factly about all these absolutely crazy things." He managed to elbow himself to a sitting position on her bed. "Tracy, what is going on?"

"Well, evidently the German espionage network knows a good deal more about our activities than we suspected," she said. "Really, no one was expecting that bundist to come snooping around last night."

"Now we've got Nazi spies?"

"We're fairly certain some of Henzler's silver-shirts are agents of the fatherland, yes," Tracy said. "We didn't think they had any inkling of what we were up to."

"They sure know more than I do. What the devil are you up to?"

"You've probably heard by now that Clifford Klaus controls the Star-Spangled Studios."

"I saw him the other . . . funny." Pete paused. "I was going to say I saw Klaus the other night at the studio, but now I'm not certain I did."

"He does visit—late in the evening usually. You could have caught a glimpse of him, though he's very discreet about it."

"Can't seem to focus my memory at all."

"Probably the aftereffect of the stun ray."

"That's what you call it? Boy, that thing really gives you a jolt and—"

"Actually, it's a good deal more humane than a conventional pistol," Tracy pointed out. "If Dangler'd used a .38 on you, you'd be in a hospital right now."

"Oh, good. Let me make a memo of that, so when Thanksgiving comes around I'll remember to say a little prayer for the bastard."

"Pete, no one wanted to hurt you." She took his hand. "This was an accident, a mistake."

"What's Klaus' part in all this?"

"Clifford Klaus is a highly eccentric man," she said. "Noted for doing things in unconventional ways. The course the world is taking, with Hitler blitzkrieging Europe, England on the edge of collapse, America likely to enter the war . . . well, Klaus feels we must have new and better weapons. That's what's being developed at the Star-Spangled warehouse."

"Why not use one of his factories? He's got 'em all over the damn country."

"He felt he'd be safer, that the chances of developing new weapons in secret would be greater if he had his staff working in an unlikely place," the girl explained. "He felt no one would suspect defense work was going on at our lot, especially since we're in the process of making a futuristic serial. Anything unusual would be written off as part of *Skyrocket Steele*."

"We really are going to make the serial, aren't we?"

"Sure, and we'll use some of the real ships and weapons in it. All safely defused of course."

"How'd the Henzler gang find out?"

"We don't know that yet."

"Are the police involved, or the FBI?"

Tracy said, "Not the local police, no. But certain key people in Washington are kept up to date on our progress."

He sat studying her for a few quiet seconds. "What you did to Dime Gallardo's car—was that a secret weapon or you?"

"That was exactly what I told you," Tracy said. "I've never lied to you."

"Well, hardly ever," he muttered.

"What?"

"Nothing—just an old punch line that popped into my head," Pete said. "Must be an after-effect."

15

SCENE 320. Interior. Palace of Emperor Borak.

SKYROCKET and BORAK face each other across the vast marble floor. SKYROCKET is looking, dismayed, at the ray gun in his hand. BORAK laughs malignantly.

BORAK

So, earthling, your ray gun is jammed!

SKYROCKET

(tossing gun aside) I don't need it, Borak! You I can handle with my fists!

BORAK

Oh, no, Skyrocket Steele. The choice of weapons shall be mine. We shall battle with . . . swords!

*　　　*　　　*

Hix appeared in the doorway. "I just knocked off the final scene for Chapter Twelve," he announced. "When we stuff in your duel pages, Pietro, we're finished."

"Another fifteen minutes and I'll have it." Hix, clutching several pages of script, came in and sat on the edge of Pete's desk. "The fadeout is absolutely brilliant," he said. "We have a clinch, with June Frenching Curly in the ear. Then we cut to the rocket ship blasting off for new adventures. Symbolic stuff worthy of Eisenstein."

"Sounds terrific."

Hix said, "I have some other stirring news for you."

"I could use some."

"Using my powers of persuasion, plus a few tricks I learned years ago in the Orient, I have convinced Owls to let you and me stay on this project another two weeks."

"Why?"

"'Why?' That's how you express boundless joy?"

"I thought I was through when the script was done. My four weeks are up tomorrow."

"They start shooting on Monday bright and early." Hix leaned toward him. "Things can go wrong—Curly may demand words of one syllable only, for instance. It's best to have two seasoned wordsmiths on hand, standing by to meet any eventuality."

"Okay, good."

Hix said, "My second wife, when she was having an affair with our Japanese gardener, acted very much the way you've been acting the past week or so."

"Don't worry—I'm not fooling around with your gardener."

"You couldn't, since the wily devil returned to the land of the rising sun over two years ago—no doubt to plot the bloody invasion of our sun-drenched shores," said Hix. "What I'm getting at, old buddy, is the fact you seem to be hiding something. I don't know if it's a secret sorrow or—"

"It has nothing to do with the script or our partnership," Pete told him. He'd promised Tracy, the morning he came to after they'd used the stun ray on him, that he wouldn't tell anyone about what he'd seen. That had turned out to be damn difficult, since he wanted very much to get Hix's ideas about the story she'd told him. "This is something personal."

"Yet your romance with the incomparable Miss Flinn seems to be blooming. I spied you holding hands at a swank nitery this past weekend," said Hix. "So what's eating on you?"

"Can't tell you right yet."

"You didn't pick up a social disease from one of the bevy of Star-Spangled starlets? I can send you to a remarkable medico in Altadena who can—"

"I remain pure as the driven snow and the Los Angeles air."

Shrugging, Hix hopped off the desk. "Well, if you're contemplating suicide, finish that scene first, huh?"

"Momentarily."

The phone rang.

Hix took it. "YWCA locker room. What can we do for you, sweetie?" he answered. "Speaking. She did? She does? So let her stew for a few . . . Me? Send Thompson, that's his . . . Threw what at him? Terrific. Then, Milton, you go next. Pile into one of your jewel-encrusted sedan chairs and order your lackies to . . . She said she'd what? Aw, June's exaggerating. . . . Likes me? Admittedly, for a bimbo with such large knockers and such a relatively small brain, she has good taste. . . . Right now? But we're winding up the script. . . . Who? Sure, I coaxed Pepita the

Mexican Pepperpot back onto the lot but that was because . . . today? For fittings and . . . Okay, okay, Milton. To hear is to obey." He spun the receiver in his hand like a six-shooter before pronging it.

"New trouble?"

"June Maze is having one of her tantrums," Hix explained. "Seems she and Gypsy Shuster had a falling out, Juney moved out and now is residing in a suite at the posh Beverly Glen Hotel. She maintains she is too distraught to return to the studio in the immediate future. Milt has to have her carcass here today for final costume fittings and some publicity stills."

"How come you're supposed to retrieve her?"

Hix growled. "Aw, I've done chores like this one before. Some of these broads find me soothing. Sort of like what a mongoose does to a snake."

"Thompson already tried?"

"Yeah, and she conked the lug with a bust of Voltaire."

"How'd June come by that?"

"Could be Gypsy won it for her at a shooting gallery." Hix walked a nervous circle in front of the bookshelves. "For all we know she has a whole set of those dornicks. Voltaire, Swift, Addison, Jonson. Probably carved from Italian marble. I don't fancy having those bounced off my sconce."

"You'll be able to soothe her."

"Come along," invited his partner.

"I ought to stick around and finish the duel."

"Listen, if Juney sulks for a few days it'll foul up production on our beloved serial," said Hix. "It's your duty to the empire, my son. Let's go."

"Okay, but I'm going to stay ducked down behind you."

16

Hix stopped dead on the sea-blue mosaic lobby tiles. "The one in the tennis togs," he said, nodding toward the nearby cocktail lounge of the air-conditioned Beverly Glen Hotel. "I'd recognize that fanny anywhere."

"I'm not a student of the subject," said Pete. "Besides which, all those outrigger canoes and rattan screens obscure the view."

"That's merely the decor of the Typhoon Room. Don't let it distract you," said Hix. "That is definitely Dorothy Lamour sitting on that bar stool."

"Even if it is, she's not the one we're here to fetch."

"I haven't seen Dot since she began her climb to stardom at Paramount." Hix moved closer to the frond-fringed doorway to the dimlit thickly decorated Typhoon Lounge. "She had a girlish crush on me back then."

"We've got to persuade June Maze to come back to—"

"I'll go in here and buy Dottie one Planter's Punch for old time's sake," Hix decided. "You forge ahead and lay the groundwork with Juney."

"I'm not the one who charmed Pepita down out of the trees. You're the Svengali of—"

"Peter, I'll join you in a matter of minutes." He gave his writing partner a helpful push between the shoulder blades. "Cottage Eleven, across the lobby and out that second door." Waiting no longer, Hix scurried into the bar.

Pete continued, pushed out into the densely cultivated garden courtyard of the hotel. There were a dozen tile-and-stucco cottages out here in the afternoon sun.

As he hunted for 11, he heard a splash to his right and realized there was a swimming pool in there amongst the palms, vines, and flowering shrubs.

He was raising his hand to take hold of the golden, shell-shaped knocker on the bright white door of Cottage 11 when he became aware of a familiar voice inside.

". . . look at dis button, will ya? Ain't dat somethin' now? Looka da way it swings back an' fort'. Dat is some union button, babe, an' it's puttin' ya right into a trance. Yeah, youse is gettin' sleepy, sleepy, sleepy . . ."

"This is no place from which to negotiate," said Hix. "Into the breach, my lad."

Blinking, Pete took hold of the knocker and used it. "How long you been standing there?"

"I only just arrived through the primeval glade," replied Hix, frowning at him. "Took me only a few moments to determine the lady was actually merely Dot Lamour's stand-in and not the genuine article. The similarity twixt the two ended at the hips. Are you okay?"

"I guess so, yeah. I must've blacked out for a minute or so."

"You really are going to have to consult a sawbones. Otherwise—"

"Yeah?" inquired a voice on the other side of the white door.

"Juney, my pet, this is Hix."

"Ya can shove it, Hix."

Hix ran his fingers through his frizzy hair. "I don't blame you for feeling punk, June," he said close to her door. "To be dropped from the Star-Spangled roster of stellar attractions right when your career was—"

"Those simps didn't drop me! Who gave ya that idea?"

"Perhaps I misunderstood. When I saw Jean Rogers being fitted for the Lucille Avon costumes this A.M., I naturally assumed—"

"Ya gotta be kidding." The door swung open and there was the platinum-blond June Maze, wearing a satin robe that was trimmed in white fur. "Who's this cluck?"

"You know Pete Tinsley, my esteemed partner on the *Skyrocket Steele* epic."

"Is he the one who wrote all the dumb lines I got?"

"Dumb lines? Dumb lines?" Hix pushed into the suite, tugging Pete along with him. "You can't be speaking of our script, honey."

"If I say stuff like that on the screen I'm gonna look like a sap." She crossed to a rattan sofa and dropped into it.

Hix and Pete watched the actress' bare thigh for a moment.

"Geeze, haven't you rubes ever seen skin before?" She rearranged the satin.

"None so stunning as yours," said Hix. "Now, Juney, maybe we can polish those lines for you. Possibly even beef up your part. What do you think, Pete?"

Pete was frowning slightly, looking around the room. All the Venetian blinds were shut and there was a musty feel. "Don't see why we ought to bother. Jean Rogers told me she thinks the Lucille Avon part is on a level with that of Scarlet—"

"That cluck." June snorted and tossed her platinum hair.

"Shoulder," warned Hix.

Tugging the satin robe back up over her bare shoulder, June said, "You and me have always been pals, Hix."

"Chums through thick and thin, yes."

"Ya gotta understand I'm going through a rough time." She brushed at her lovely nose with a lacy handkerchief she produced out of her bosom. "Gypsy may be a lousy rat and a rotten crook to boot, but I sorta loved the guy."

"Love is funny that way." Hix gave her a sympathetic smile and settled on the edge of the couch. "Ouch!"

"Ya sat on my pin cushion, ya sap."

Rising briefly, Hix removed the heart-shaped cushion. "I truly think, June, that if you blow your nose, dry your great big beautiful eyes and powder that pretty face of yours—why, we can escort you right back to Star-Spangled to—"

"They can kiss my behind."

Pete asked, "Is someone else here?"

"What gives ya that idea? I ain't one of those persons who shacks up with a bunch of—"

"Cigar butt in the ashtray." He nodded at the silver tray on the wicker coffee table.

June stared at it. "How the Jesus did that get here? I ain't had anybody in here except the maid, and she wasn't puffing on no stogies."

"We'll complain to the management when we depart," promised Hix. "The important thing, June, is to reinstate you with Milt."

"That jerk." She folded her arms, causing the robe to slip off both shoulders.

"Shoulders," said Hix.

"To hell with it—let 'em show," said the actress. "The way I see this, Hix, it ain't me who has to apologize. See, I telephoned

Thompson to tell him how I was heartbroken at the moment and couldn't go before the cameras for a couple days. That bastard tells me tough tiddy and I better get my buns over there to the lot pronto. Such crust."

"Thompson is a businessman, not an artist," said Hix.

"Ya can say that again. Him and Milt Owls are money-grubbing bastards."

"You and I and Pete are all fellow artists. We all realize you're exactly right for the Lucille part," Hix told her. "Naturally we don't want to see our masterpiece fouled up with Constance Moore taking over the part of—"

"I thought you said it was that insipid Jean Rogers who was stealing my part."

"She's the first in line, yes," Hix said quickly. "However, Connie Moore's got quite a reputation for handling exactly this sort of demanding role."

"A cold potato," said June. "She ain't got oomph— or tits."

"Still, Milt and Thompson think—"

"When Thompson finally comes over to talk to me here, instead of being sympathetic, the bastard tries to make a pass," said June, nostrils flaring. "I fixed his wagon. Do you know how many stitches it took to patch up his coco?"

"Nine." Pete moved to the door. "Maybe we ought to leave June to her sorrow and go with Jean—"

"I'd like to see that broad handle the slime people scene. Fooey."

Hix said, "If we rush you back to the studio, June, we can guarantee you'll keep the part."

The blond actress sighed. "I tell ya, Hix, I am going sorta stir crazy in this joint," she said. "All that jungle out there—it's like living in a damn Hunneker movie."

Hix put an arm around her bare shoulders. "Get dressed and we'll sneak you back."

"Oh, Hix, I really loved that Gypsy mug." Sobbing, she put her arms around him and hugged.

Over her head, Hix narrowed one eye and nodded at the door. "You can drive on back to SS, Pietro," he said. "I'll see to it June is safely delivered."

"Nobody understands what stardom means," said the crying girl. "The pressures, the pains."

"I know." Hix rubbed her smooth white back.

"See you later, folks." Pete left.

Outside, he started across the courtyard. There was a sudden rustling in the underbrush a few yards from the actress's cottage.

"Hey, who's there?"

Pete ran to the spot where he'd seen the movement.

There was no one there.

17

The velvety night sky was rich with sparkling stars; they seemed very close to the observatory. Shivering, Lucille Avon turned to her gray-haired old father. Slender fingers toying with the collar of her crepe dress, she said, "But, Father, Sky's seldom wrong when it comes to astronomical matters."

"I know, my child—yet what you two are suggesting is . . . incredible to say the least." Professor Avon, his rumpled white lab coat pockets laden with bits of paper and small scientific instruments, came shuffling over to where his lovely blonde daughter stood next to the handsome Skyrocket Steele.

"What's happening is incredible, Prof," said Skyrocket. "Which is why we've summoned you back to your observatory at this late hour."

"Very well, Skyrocket, very well." The old scientist moved to the eyepiece of the gigantic telescope. "Move aside, Lucille dear, and let your father take a look."

"Father, our world is doomed!" gasped Lucille. "The moon is hurtling straight for Earth at a rate of . . . Hot damn! The old goat did it again!"

"Merely a fatherly pat, my child."

"Ya got to keep this rumhead from goosing me!" June Maze, out of character and hands on hips, turned to scowl at the director.

"Monte, I don't like to do more than one take," said the small, frail young director from the edge of the set. "We've done three already. Please, Monte, as a favor to me, don't fondle June's buttocks when you gaze heavenward."

"Rex, you have the word of a seasoned trouper, 'twas no more than a cordial pat." Monte Nightbridge, smiling innocently and eyeing the star-studded ceiling of the observatory set, raised his right hand like a witness taking the oath.

"He goosed me," reiterated June, rubbing her backside. "I've had a lot of fatherly pats in my day, buster, and I know a goose when I feel one."

"Better," suggested the handsome Curly Horner, "get down to business, Monte."

"I don't expect you, Curlilocks, to appreciate the nuances of a performance," said Nightbridge, "but June, my child, surely an actress of your capability must realize—"

"You goose me once more, I'll boot you in the nuts."

"Monte," said Rex Ireland from his canvas director's chair, "what is that I notice in your lower right-hand pocket?"

"A slide rule, my boy."

"A slide rule doesn't slosh." The thin young man touched at the frames of his glasses. "That other thing is what I mean."

"Ah, yes, it's a beaker flask," explained the gray-haired actor. "It adds authenticity to my attire. A scientific touch."

"What's in it, Monte?"

Nightbridge's eyebrows climbed and fluttered. "I hesitate to reply with ladies about, Rex." He hoisted the glass flask out of the lab coat pocket. "The fact is I promised to deliver a urine sample to the Burbank Memorial Hospital this afternoon and, wishing to kill two birds with one stone, I brought—"

"That urine looks very much like bourbon from here," said Ireland.

"You've noticed that, too? Yes, that's one of the reasons I'm anxious to consult an expert medical man to—"

"Monte, you promised me. Your lamebrained agent promised me. The Star-Spangled contract spelled it all out in language even an actor can understand."

Nightbridge rotated the flask and the amber liquid made a gurgle sound. "No booze," he said quietly.

"No booze, that's right. Not a drop is to be consumed by you anywhere near my sets." Slowly, the young director stood and removed his glasses.

"Watch this," said Hix to Pete.

The two writers were standing in the shadows beyond the brightly lit set.

Pete asked, "Is he going to do the glasses business? I've heard about it."

"Exactly, you are about to witness the famous Rex Ireland glasses routine."

"Monte, I've been directing chapter plays at Star-Spangled since I was seventeen," said the twenty-three-year-old director. "I'm noted for my even temper, my keen sense of pace and action, my ability to shoot *always* under budget. I seldom lose my temper, unless one of my people does some little thing that'll make us go *over* budget. When that happens I . . . *Aaaaiiii! Aaaarrrgghhh!* Yow! Yow! Yow!"

Young Ireland tore off his glasses, threw them to the sound stage floor, and began dancing on them with his sneakered feet. The lenses crackled and clacked.

From a dark place off to the right of the director's chair emerged a slim girl in a navy blue skirt and crisp white blouse. She handed him a fresh pair of glasses and returned into the darkness.

"I hope I won't have to lose my temper again today." Ireland put the spectacles on. "Monte, turn that flask over to one of the grips and we'll do the scene once more. *Once.*"

"Brilliant, Rex." Nightbridge sauntered to the edge of the set to pass his flask over to a thickset man in coveralls. "Your performance grows more daring each time I see it—bids fair to rival my own legendary nineteen twenty-eight enacting of Hamlet on Broadway."

"Let us slip away before they start shooting again," whispered Hix. "I could do with some lunch."

The director resumed his canvas chair. "This time I want Curly standing between June and you, Monte."

"Going to make it difficult to deliver that friendly pat on the—"

"There isn't going to be any pat, Monte. For if there is, another grand old actor, Francis X. Bushman, will be wearing the smock when shooting resumes."

"Bushman. A second-rate ham."

Pete followed his partner over the strewn cables and wires and out into the bright midday. "Does it always go so slow?"

"Rex is a damn good director, and fast as hell." Hix squinted in the sunlight. "First day he usually lets them fool around some. Then he really starts cracking down. I've known him to go through six pairs of specs in a single afternoon."

"Expensive."

"Naw, they're all window glass. Nothing wrong with his eyes," said Hix. "Want to try the commissary? I believe the girls from the sultan's harem in *Spawn of the Sands* will be dining there about now."

"Sure, might as well. I'd like to get back quick and watch some more of the filming." They started in the direction of the studio dining rooms. "How come you're ogling—doesn't your heart belong to Boots?"

"Yes, there's a great and lasting romance in the making," replied Hix. "As far as the Hix heart goes, it belongs to Boots McKay and no other. Other parts of my anatomy, however, are not as yet spoken for. You know, there's one girl in that harem who is fully six feet tall and yet perfectly proportioned so that . . . Oh, boy!" He pointed excitedly.

Pete turned. "Hey, the prop warehouse is open."

Hix grabbed Pete's arm. "We'll peek."

"Maybe we ought to wait until—"

"Nix on that. We're going to feast our eyes right now, sonny boy."

There was a deserted pickup parked near the open rear door of the forbidden warehouse. No one—neither guard nor workman—was visible inside the warehouse or out.

Immediately across the threshold were rows of work-benches. Looming large beyond them were six huge spaceships.

"Look at these nifty ray guns." Hix dashed to the nearest table to snatch up a Silver weapon. "Yeah, this is quite handsome, beats anything Buster Crabbe ever waved around." He spun suddenly, aimed the pistol at Pete. "Your end is nigh, Emperor Borak."

"Hix, for Christ sake, don't—"

ZZZZZUUUUUMMMMM!

The frizzle-haired writer had squeezed the trigger.

Pete was in the act of throwing himself to the concrete floor when the beam of light from the gun swept over him.

He hit the floor hard, rattling his teeth, bunging up his elbow. He realized that the gun had been deactivated and was now harmless. Shaking his head and rubbing at his sore arm, he got to his feet.

Hix, ray gun dangling in his hand, was staring at him. "What the hell was that all about?"

"Nothing. Guess I'm a bit nervous."

"Have you thought about switching to Postum?" said Hix.

18

The stuntman tossed away his cigarette. It came arcing down across the clear afternoon to sputter out in the yellow sand surrounding the spaceship.

"These frigging things better work this time," said Bud Duttlinger from atop the spaceship as two crewmen readjusted the flying belt rockets on his back. "All you got to do is make a little frigging smoke come out."

"They'll work, they'll work, trust me," said the second unit director from the ground. He was a weathered man of sixty, dressed in faded cowboy clothes.

The crewmen hooked Duttlinger into the harness, then got him dangling properly alongside the spaceship on the slanting wires. Duttlinger stretched out his arms in front of him. He was dressed in a facsimile of Curly Horner's costume—black boots, white trousers, and a dark jersey with a silver collar studded with a dozen mock bolts. He wore a fairly believable platinum wig.

"What they'll do," explained Tracy, "is let him slide down the two wires to the ground."

Pete said, "Won't the wires show?"

"Not in the finished sequence, no," the girl answered. "When they run the footage backwards, it'll look just like Bud's flying up from the sand to the top of the rocket."

"Nothing is what it seems." Pete was standing on the warm sand beside Tracy, beyond the ring of technicians who were setting up the flying sequences.

"Do I sense a double meaning?"

"From me? Shucks, ma'am, I'm merely a wide-eyed yokel," he said. "Up until we came out here to the desert, I didn't even know Skyrocket needed wires before he could fly."

"Sometimes I think maybe too much of Hix's cockiness is rubbing off on you."

"You frigging idiots!" bellowed Duttlinger.

"You wanted smoke, you got smoke."

The stuntman and the two crewmen were engulfed in swirls of yellow smoke.

"If it weren't for Hix," said Pete as he turned away from the rocket ship to follow the departing girl, "I wouldn't even be out here in the vicinity of Palm Springs. He wangled yet another two weeks out of Owls."

"You've been very useful on the rewrites and all." She walked slowly across the sand. "If you weren't good, even the glib Mr. Hix couldn't talk Milton into keeping you on."

"Hix is a bright guy," said Pete. "For instance, he's smart enough to know I'm not leveling with him."

"About what, us? You two aren't sorority sisters, you know, you don't have to confess every little—"

"I'm talking about this defense work or whatever it is. Seems to me, Tracy, it wouldn't do any harm if I told—"

"No, you're not to tell him anything." She halted near a shaggy Joshua tree, faced him. The bent-elbow branches threw zigzag shadows across her. "That would only make trouble."

"Not telling the truth bothers me. Acting and pretending makes me uneasy."

"Then maybe you're in the wrong line of work," she told him. "Maybe you ought to go back to writing tripe for those lurid maga—"

"I don't write tripe," he said evenly. "How would you know anyway? You've never read a word of anything of mine. You—"

"Please, Pete, don't turn into an egomaniac. I've got enough of them to contend with already." She took his hand. "I like you. It has nothing to do with what you do for a living. Okay?"

After a few seconds he answered, "Okay, sure."

"Good. Now I have to get over to Curly's cottage," she said, withdrawing her hand. "We've got to fit in a couple of fan magazine interviews this afternoon. If I possibly can, we'll have lunch."

He watched her hurry away across the desert toward the scatter of tourist cabins the location company had taken over.

"Terrific! Now slowly turn around toward the camera and let's see a tear or two come trickling down your boyish cheek as we dolly in for a tight close-up." Hix, clad in an explosive Hawaiian shirt and white tennis shorts, was making his way across the sand.

"Your condolences are appreciated," said Pete. "Just arising?"

"I'm a victim of love, my lad," said the frizzy-haired writer. "Courting the incomparable Boots in far-off Hollywood each night and then zooming back across the moon swept desert sands to Palm Springs each morn is wearing me down. Even a man of my iron constitution finds it hard to revive much before ten in the A.M."

"I was watching them do some of the flying-belt stuff."

Hix, eyebrows dipping, took his partner by the arm. "Listen, Petrov," he said in a confiding tone, "I may have made a truly startling discovery."

"About Boots?"

"Nay. This has nothing to do with the romance of Hix," he said. "This pertains to what is being built in yon warehouses." He gestured at the two large stucco-and-aluminum buildings. that had been constructed in the desert some two hundred yards from the cabins.

"They're just building more props for our serial."

Hix said, "Pedro, them things ain't just for our fillum."

Pete stumbled. "Oops."

"What'd you trip on?"

"Nothing. I don't know. A snake or something. Go on."

"Slip into my cabana," said Hix, "and I shall tell all."

*   *   *

Bouncing on the edge of his unmade bed, Hix said, "I saw it with these very eyes."

"There could be another explanation." Pete was sitting uneasily in a mission-style chair.

Cupping a hand to his ear, Hix invited, "Lay it on me."

"Well, they could've been testing the rocket ships."

"Testing 'em?" Hix bounced to his feet. "Lad, I saw one of them blimp-size babies come floating out of the open warehouse to settle on the flatbed of an enormous truck. It was flying! Do you comprehend what I am babbling about? The dang thing can actually fly through the air with the greatest of ease. Even though it is but a prop, a thing of fantasy, it really and truly does fly."

"Our budget is large enough so that—"

"Horse crap!" Hix strode closer, pointed at his partner. "I hauled home here last night at three A.M. Unable to sleep, since my little heart was aflutter with romantic notions and postcoital euphoria, I decided to take a stroll out in the sands of the desert. It's always nice to pad across the sand and maybe take a leak against a cactus plant. But I never got me member all the way out of me fly. No, because I beheld this warehouse, the one on the left, slide open. Then, as I stood dumbfounded, my gifted fingers still clutching my infamous dork, one of our supposedly prop rocket ships flew out and got aboard that damn truck. As I stood there, trying to look as much like a Joshua tree as I could, I witnessed fully three—count 'em, three—of the spaceships come flying out to settle onto trucks. Then the warehouse silently shut up and the trucks went rolling away to lord knows where."

"Owls is probably having some of them brought back to Burbank for—"

"Pete, cease playing dumb," advised Hix. "You know darn well those ships are just to look at—they don't fly. Any flying will be done in miniature, using the models Owls is allowing Muldow and his minions to build."

Pete tapped his fingers on the wooden arm of his chair. "Maybe I better tell you something."

"Do you know what the hell is going on? You've been acting like a high school lass auditioning for a part in the remake of *Mata Hari* of late, but I thought perhaps that was nothing more than a side effect of your torrid romance with Tracy."

"You have to promise not to tell anyone else about this."

Hix drew ah *X* over his abdomen. "Cross m'heart," he said. "Now give."

"Well, it has to do with the safety of the country, more or less."

One eyebrow lifted. "Oh, so?"

"See, Clifford Klaus is sort of eccentric," began Pete. He recounted to Hix the explanation Tracy had given him for what was actually going on.

When he finished, Hix said, "And you swallowed all that guff?"

Pete stood, angry. "Tracy doesn't lie to me."

Hix took two backward steps. "Sure?"

Pete hesitated before answering, "Yeah, I'm sure."

19

The moonlight made the Martian temple seem real. Pete glanced at it as he sneaked by, almost expecting Emperor Borak to come storming out between the pillars and down the wide stone stairway.

Stationing himself next to a tall, thick cactus, Pete settled down on the cooling sand. From here he could watch the warehouses. Last night Pete had been here, too, but there'd been no activity. He believed in Tracy, didn't think she was lying to him, yet he wanted to see what was going on.

It was after midnight and the wind drifting across the desert was cool.

Sitting with his arms hugging his knees, he went over in his head the scene he had to revise for tomorrow's shooting.

*　　*　　*

SCENE 102. Exterior. Martian temple.

The horde of six-armed Martian warriors drag the struggling LUCILLE up to the steps of the temple.

LUCILLE

You'll never get away with this!

WARRIOR CHIEF

Silence, wench!

LUCILLE

Skyrocket Steele won't allow you to sacrifice me to your pagan gods!

WARRIOR CHIEF

(laughing maliciously) Foolish girl! Don't you know that Skyrocket Steele is dead?

*　　*　　*

"Psst."

Pete sat up straight, causing his back to come into sudden contact with the prickly base of the big cactus. "What's up?"

Hix, crouched low, was coming across the night sand toward him. "I've been hunting around for you for nigh on to fifteen minutes, pard."

"Thought you were seeing Boots tonight."

"I was, I did," replied Hix. "Which is why, once I heard the startling news she had for me, I came highballing back here."

"What's wrong? I heard Henzler's silver-shirts were holding a rally over in Manzana, and that's only twenty miles or so from here. Are they going to make a stab at swiping the—"

"Forget the Secret Agent X-9 crap for the nonce," Hix told him. "Boots, even though she is definitely signed for a fat part in *Dancing Coeds*, still likes to augment her income in ways I don't quite approve of."

"She's still dancing at stag parties?"

"Last night she was hired to entertain at a gathering in Santa Monica, a get-together of movie bigwigs and gangland luminaries. Okay, so there is Boots inside this huge cake. They have wheeled her in and whilst she awaits her cue to burst forth, she happens to overhear a conversation that is taking place between some old chums of ours. Namely, Gypsy Shuster and Dime Gallardo."

"Dime's supposed to be in the hosp—"

"He's out on crutches, as nasty as ever," said Hix. "What Boots overhears these heavies plotting is this. Gypsy wants June Maze back and he is prepared to go to considerable trouble to get her."

"You mean he's going to come out here to grab her?"

"Precisely. Gypsy Shuster, in the company of a sufficient number of goons, intends to raid us. He'll glom dear Juney, drag her across the border into some dingy Nevada town, and have a crooked justice of the peace splice 'em."

"That violates at least two or three laws," said Pete. "When does he strike?"

Hix sighed. "Boots had to pop up out of the frosting and start shimmying at that point," he explained. "But she thinks these hoodlums will hit us either tonight or tomorrow night."

Standing, Pete said, "We'd better warn June, and our security people."

"You alert the guards, I'll inform June." Hix brushed sand from his plaid slacks. "Then meet me back at my digs in one half hour."

"It's going to take you a half hour just to—"

"The poor kid may need a little consoling." Hix gave a mock salute and went jogging off across the sand.

Pete was about to follow when a fleeting glimmer of light near one of the prop warehouses distracted him. Hunching slightly, he squinted toward the flicker.

Nothing now.

"Better check on it." He ran in the direction of the warehouse.

When he was still a dozen yards away, he slowed to a stop.

The front door of the domed building had been pulled halfway open. Lying flat out in the opening was a man in a guard uniform.

Turning on his heel, Pete ran back for the cottages. This was something Tracy had to know about.

He never reached her cottage.

Approaching it from the rear, Pete saw a dark figure lumbering away from her back door. Tracy, obviously out cold, was draped over the figure's broad padded shoulder.

"Hey," shouted Pete, "what the hell are you doing?"

Then he noticed Dime Gallardo.

The gangster, leg in a cast, was standing in a strip of moonlight next to the girl's cabin. "Ah, my old pal, the punk," he chuckled.

"You're supposed to be snatching June." He moved for the hoodlum.

"That's Gyp's business. Me, I'm picking up a little something for myself."

"No, I don't think so." Pete dived at him.

Laughing, Dime swung out with his crutch.

The padded armrest took Pete full in the chin.

He bit his tongue, yowled, went stumbling back.

He didn't see the second blow—only heard it come whistling down through the darkness.

20

"... and so Lord Brett is faced with the troubling question of whether or not he can trust this mysterious girl. He is also puzzled by the sudden disappearance of both Agatha and her wheelchair. Perhaps we'll learn the answers to these and other questions which face Lord Brett on 'The Path to Love.' But first we've got a date in the spankin' clean Super Lard kitchen, where Aunt Betty's going to show the always hungry Denny how to make codfish balls so they come out so crispy you ..."

Morning sunlight touched Pete's face, along with someone's fingers.

"I was really stupid," said Tracy, whose fingers they were. "I should've sensed their approach. Sometimes, though, I don't get any warning at all. So they got the drop on me, managed to give me a shot of something that knocked me flat. Are you okay?"

He reflected on the question. "Guess so," he answered. "Dime bopped me on the head with his crutch. How long have I been out?"

"All night. I think they gave you a shot of something, too," said the girl.

Pete was stretched out on a twin bed, rustic wooden walls surrounded him. The small, high, screened windows showed pine trees outside. "Any notion whereabouts we are?"

"Out of the state," answered Tracy. "I only just came to myself."

"... Yum, that's sure flaky and good, Aunt Betty."

"Good for you, too, Denny. And anybody can fry up a batch of crisp, mouth-waterin' codfish balls if they just make sure they always fry in nothing but Super Lard, the ..."

"Where's the radio?"

Tracy nodded toward a closed doorway. "Next room. Being listened to by a lout with a .45 automatic in his armpit."

"This must be Nevada." Pete sat up. "That's where Gypsy was going to drag June."

From the other twin bed came an annoyed moan. "Louse," muttered the awakening actress. "So-and-so...."

"Take it easy, June," said Tracy, turning to her.

"Stick a needle in my fanny, will he! That slob." She was wide-awake now, pouting. "Such crust. Who the hell does he think he is! Why, for two bits and change I'd—"

"Hey, you bimbos! Shut up in there!" The bedroom door was yanked open and a thickset man in a checkered suit glared in. "I can't hear my frigging broadcast."

"Monk?" June swung off the bed walked, tottering some, to the open doorway. "You got some nerve, helping that low-life Gypsy to kidnap me. Wasn't I always nice to ya?"

"Don't make me feel like a rat, Juney."

"You are a rat! You and that boss of yours are both crums!"

"Aw, I wish you wouldn't take it that way, kid." Monk rubbed at his flattened nose. "I'm only doing my job."

"What's Gyp have in mind anyhow? He ain't going to keep me cooped up in this dump too long or I'll start howlin' like a stuck pig."

"He's going to marry you," explained Monk. "We're waiting for the Reverend Josiah Hornbloom of the Wayside Church of the Holy Voices to pedal up here from Arendsville. Arendsville is a quaint little burg down the hill from this lodge."

"Pedal?"

"The old geek insisted on coming on his bicycle," explained the hoodlum. "He won't get in an auto for nothing. Claims the holy voices warned him about the combustion engine."

"Wow, that's absolutely great," said the angry actress. "Not bad enough I get kidnapped, but now my wedding's gonna feature some old coot who hears voices."

"You coulda had a nice church wedding," reminded Monk. "But you took a powder, kid."

"Listen, I ain't gonna tie up with Gypsy Shuster! Now or ever!" shouted June. "I got real star potential and I ain't gonna hitch my wagon to a cheap hood."

"You shouldn't ought to talk about your prospective groom that way," warned Monk. "It's bad luck."

"Where is the lug? I'll tell him to his ugly face."

"He's in the cabin next door, but he ain't up yet, Juney . . ."

Easing off the bed, Pete moved close to Tracy. "We have another problem," he said quietly, "besides Gypsy and Dime."

"What?"

"Right before I came over to your cabin last night, I spotted trouble in one of the desert prop warehouses," he said. "It was open, the guard was unconscious on the threshold. Rather than barge in, I decided to go fetch you. I wanted to avoid getting stunned or—"

"Damn! I'm going to have to get back there right away!"

"You figure the Nazis made a try to—"

"No, it's worse than that."

"Worse? What's worse than the Nazis? You mean the Japs?"

"I was hoping to talk us out of this mess here." She rubbed at her wrist, glancing around the rustic cabin. "That'll take too long. I'm going to have to tip my hand."

"You're going to use your . . . knacks?"

Nodding, Tracy said, "Yes. I'll have to take drastic steps—there's no time for diplomacy. Be ready to follow my lead."

"Don't do that. I don't want to smack you, kid," Monk was saying to the angry June.

"Ya creepy moron!" She was drumming on his broad chest with both fists. "Ya dumb putz!"

"Take it easy, Juney, else I'll . . . ooof!" Monk straightened up like a soldier coming to attention. Then his arms flapped up, his automatic climbed out of his holster and flew across the rustic living room. Eyes snapping shut, he went limp and tumbled over onto the Navajo rug.

June turned from the fallen thug to stare at Tracy and Pete. "What the heck is going on?" she asked. "Did ya have something to do with this? I mean, what the dickens is . . . ooof." She fell over sideways, landing atop Monk.

"Why her?" Pete asked.

"I have to concentrate to get us out of here quick." Tracy walked into the living room of the cabin. "Babbling distracts me. Be easier to carry her out anyway. Pick her up, will you?"

"Sure, okay." He bent, gathered up the actress, and arranged her over his shoulder.

Stopped in the living room, Tracy was frowning.

"Okay. I sense that Gypsy and Dime are still asleep in the cabin next to this one," she said. "There are two hoods on guard outside, though."

Pete got hold of the knob of the outer door, turned it carefully. "This is locked. Probably Monk has the—"

"Stand back a minute."

Shifting June's weight, he backed a few steps.

Tracy raised her right hand, pointed at the heavy wooden door.

There was a metallic shriek. The door went ripping free of its hinges and sailed out into the morning.

"Jumpin' catfish!" exclaimed someone outside.

Tracy laughed. "Excuse it. I like to show off now and then," she said. "Don't go out yet."

"What about you? Those heavies have got guns."

Tracy was framed in the opening, where the oaken door had been. "Hey, you guys, I want that white car there," she called to one of the gangsters. "The sports job. Bring it over."

"Are you nuts, babe? Get your butt back inside . . . yowie!"

Pete, weighed down with the platinum-haired actress, reached the doorway in time to witness the flight of the hood into the pine trees.

His companion, a small man in a pinstripe suit, tried to duck behind the car Tracy'd requested and yank a weapon out of his shoulder holster. He was still lowering into a squat and clutching at the handle of the gun when she caused him to rise a rapid thirty feet into the air.

He remained there for a second before executing a shaky loop which carried him clear over the nearest treetops.

The white, top-down roadster came rolling up to the porch of the cabin.

"Let's go." Tracy stepped outside. "Be safer with the top up."

All by itself the canvas top rose up and clicked into place.

"You drive," the girl said. "Dump June in the back seat."

Pete started around the nose of the machine. "Your knack is a lot more—"

"Don't you never learn, punk."

A grinning Dime Gallardo was hobbling toward him.

"No time to be a sport," Pete said. Ducking low, careful not to drop the unconscious June, he lunged and kicked.

His foot connected with the tip of Dime's crutch. Before the gangster could pull his gun from his pocket, he fell over backwards into a clump of weeds. "Kick a cripple, huh? Boy, what kind of guy are you?" The weight of his cast kept him from rising.

Depositing June in the rear seat of the roadster, Pete jumped into the front seat and took hold of the steering wheel. "No keys."

Tracy was already in the passenger seat. "We don't need them." She gestured at the dashboard.

The engine came purring to life.

Pete released the hand brake, put the machine into gear, and slammed his foot down on the gas pedal. "That looks like the road we want through the pines there."

"Yep—that'll get us to Arendsville at least."

"Hey, where do you slobs think you're going?" A dark lean man in a bright kimono came running out of the other cabin with a .45 automatic in each hand.

"Gypsy Shuster," said Pete.

Blam!

A slug smacked into the windshield, making ragged spiderwebs.

"I'll handle this one," said Tracy.

Gypsy was running toward them, guns blazing.

Tracy cocked a finger.

The gangster executed a perfect somersault, silken robe flapping like wings.

Not exactly perfect, since he whacked his head hard into a rock on landing.

Pete saw the end of the flight in the rearview mirror, having swung the roadster around and headed it for the way off the hill.

When he returned his full attention to the road he noted a startled old man on a bicycle directly in his path.

"Out of our way, please," suggested Tracy.

The Reverend Josiah Hornbloom of the Wayside Church of the Holy Voices, as well as his blue bicycle, rose ten feet straight up off the dusty road.

"That'll give him something," said Pete, "to talk over with his voices."

"The old gentleman'll no doubt pass it off as a miracle."

When they reached the road to town, Pete said, "Don't see any sign of pursuit."

"They can't follow," said the girl. "I took the spark plugs out of the other two cars."

"You did that by remote control?"

"Yep." She folded her arms under her breasts, leaned back against the leather seat.

Pete concentrated on guiding the car along the tree-lined country road for a few minutes. "Tracy," he said finally, "you better tell me what's going on."

Looking straight ahead, she replied, "Yes, I suppose I must."

21

"Maybe reclusive millionaires and their staffs can invent stun-ray pistols that really stun and rocket ships that really rocket," said Pete. "There's a lot more than that involved here, though, Tracy. Some of what you did back there at the crooks' hideout I can't even begin to understand."

They were driving through the small Nevada town of Arendsville. It was exactly six blocks long, all one- and two-story buildings—a general store, a hardware store, three saloons, a saddle shop, a barber. Weather-beaten men in jeans and flannel shirts moved along its streets, thin women in faded housedresses.

"Turn right at the next corner," said Tracy, "that'll put us on the road back to Palm Springs."

"I saw the sign," he said. "You were going to provide an explanation."

Turning, Tracy glanced into the back seat at the still-out-cold June Maze. "You've probably suspected," she said, "that up to now I haven't been absolutely open and truthful with you."

"I've tried to believe you," he told her. "Except . . ."

"I wanted to confide in you a long time ago." She moved closer to him on the auto seat. "If it were only up to me, I would've. You have to believe, hold on to the fact that I . . . that I'm in love with you."

"I've been in love with you . . ." He let the sentence trail off. "Christ, everything serious comes out like bad movie dialogue. The thing is, Tracy, I really have been in love with you since that first crazy night at the Zig Zag."

"Me, too," she said. "Although, we aren't supposed to let anything like this happen. We didn't calculate that—"

"You keep saying we. Who exactly is we?"

"I'll get to that," she promised. "You'll be meeting most of them if you're going to help me get our weapons back. Drive a bit faster, by the way."

He accelerated the white sports car. "Can't the FBI or your Washington connections help . . . Yeah, but wait. There aren't any Washington connections, are there? That was part of the con you handed me."

"Yes, that's right."

"But you aren't a . . . a German agent? No, I can't believe I'm in love with a saboteur."

"No, I'm not," she said. "This isn't a simple domestic mess I've gotten you tangled into."

"What do you mean by domestic?"

"I mean a problem that has to do only with Earth. You see, it wasn't only Henzler's people who've been snooping around. We're certain of that now, and I'm afraid they've made a move sooner than we expected," Tracy said. "We let you believe it was only Nazis, to keep you from talking until we were ready."

"Ready for what?"

"Let me try to explain. Pete, you've written a lot about life on other planets—at least those in your own immediate system. The idea of extraterrestrial life shouldn't be very unsettling to you."

He said, "I don't really know if I believe in that or not. My idea of what life on Venus or Mars is like comes more from other pulp stories than from any sound scientific knowledge. For all you could prove by me, there isn't any life on . . . Holy Christ! I see what you're leading up to. Except that's . . . not possible."

"It is, though," she assured him. "As far as your Solar System is concerned, there is no intelligent life of any sort on any planet except this one. Beyond your little system, though, there are many others. In the system I come from there is humanoid life on several of the planets. Our problem has been that even with a number of habitable worlds, the incredible population growth is—"

"Whoa now. You really are telling me you . . . come from another planet?"

"It's name is Esmeralda," she answered. "I left there when I was, in Earth reckoning, thirteen years old."

"Left to come here?"

"Yes."

"How, by rocket ship?"

"That would have taken much too long, considering the location of Esmeralda. We used a method which utilizes teleportation and a knowledge of the space-time continuum."

"Oh, I see." He realized he was breathing rapidly, but outside of that was taking all this very well.

"There were ten of us in the original takeover study unit," Tracy went on. "All of us have the same special abilities you've seen me use. Actually—"

"What's a takeover study unit?"

She looked out at the road, at the grassy fields. "Well, Esmeralda is interested in colonizing planets in various systems, planets with comparable life-supporting conditions," she said. "The rapid population growth makes that essential to us, especially since we prefer planet life to that in artificial colonies."

"Sure, that makes sense," he said. "What you're saying is you're an invader from another planet."

"We came initially to study Earth, to determine whether it was worth taking over."

"You've apparently decided it is. Otherwise why build all the weapons?"

"Over a year ago it was agreed that Earth might be taken over," Tracy said. "Our experience has been that, even with our extra abilities and knacks, we'll need weapons when we finally move to annex your planet. We had to work out a way to build enough ships and guns to provide the others when they arrive."

"And when do the rest of 'em arrive?"

"When we send the signal. At the rate we're building up a supply of weapons, I'd say we'll be ready for your planet in another year or less."

"My planet," murmured Pete.

"Based on past annexations, it was decided it's easier to build here on the site rather than bringing everything in," Tracy continued. "In a war-torn or about to be war-torn world it's difficult to start producing quantities of guns and flying ships without attracting attention. Here in America agencies such as the FBI would probably soon find out about it. Unless—"

"Unless you had an innocent explanation for what you were doing," said Pete. "That's how come *Skyrocket Steele*. You announce you're going to produce a scientific adventure serial. You start building rockets, ray guns—the works. Hardly anybody, outside of Roscoe Muldow's union, thinks twice about what you're up to. Just another grandiose Hollywood gimmick—full-size props and realistic ray guns."

"That was the plan, yes."

"So how much longer do I have to work as a screenwriter before I become a slave of you Esmeraldans?" A year did you say?"

"Pete, it won't be like that." She took hold of his arm. "Really, we aren't like Hitler or—"

"Oh, good. No whips and chains? No pogroms or concentration camps? That's nice to know. Of course, since I've got an in with the management I'll probably get preferential treatment anyway. A bigger cell maybe, or do you folks use pens? No matter, I'm sure we'll all—"

"Listen to me, damn it. We don't do things like that. There'll be a takeover, of course, but—"

"Hey, I just realized who we is," he cut in. "Owls has to be one of you, right? Yeah—there's no other way you could bring this off without him. Imagine, Milton Owls is from another planet. Klaus, too. The reclusive millionaire has to be one of your boys."

"That's right, yes. With our intelligence and extra abilities, it wasn't too tough to rise in your society. Clifford has done remarkably well, as has Milton. Star-Spangled really is a very successful operation."

"How about Thompson? He part of the bunch?"

Tracy nodded. "He's . . . well in Earth terms he'd be my uncle."

"An uncle, good," he said. "Usually they say the guy's a cousin. Let's see now. Couple of the studio guards must be Esmeraldans. Or do you call yourselves Esmeraldians? I never can get that right. Makes no difference since . . . Hey! Not Hix?" He hit the brakes. The roadster quivered to a jolting stop. "Don't tell me Hix is one of you?"

"No, he's one of you."

Pete sighed out a breath. "So there's still somebody I can trust."

"You can trust me," she said. "Now, Pete, I really want to get back to Palm Springs to see what's been happening."

He got the car moving again. "Nice of you to give me the chance to be a collaborator. Or is traitor the word?"

"Pete, I know this is a very unusual situation for you, but—"

"Unusual?" He let out a wild, whooping laugh. "That has got to be the understatement of the decade. Jesus, I fall in love with you and you start throwing hoodlums around in the air and then it's big heavy cars and doors and men of the cloth on bicycles. I was just getting used to the idea that I was crazy about a girl who can do that sort of thing," he told her. "Now you want me to sell out my country . . . No, sell out my whole damn planet. I really do love you, Tracy, but I don't think I can do it."

She said, "I'm sorry."

"Sorry doesn't quite cover it."

"As bad as you think things may be with us, they'll be damn worse with the Peregrinians."

He almost drove off the road. When he had the car under control, he managed to say, "There's another alien invader to worry about?"

"Peregrine is another planet in our system."

"You know, I had an aunt back in East Moline who always warned me I'd damage my mind if I kept writing for the pulps," he said. "Could be she was absolutely correct. I can't—"

"The Peregrinians have similar powers," said Tracy. "But they're much more ruthless in their conquests of new planets. You see, one of our problems is to colonize a planet and at the same time keep the Peregrinians out. We've suspected for the past year they had agents here on Earth."

"So it'd be to my advantage to work for a takeover by your team?"

"There's no doubt of it," Tracy said, leaning anxiously forward. "I'm worried they may have destroyed our warehouses at Palm Springs. Either that or stolen the weapons."

"That'd be a real pity."

"It would, honestly. You don't know what they're like. Earth under their rule would be terrible," she said. "We'll check on the situation in Palm Springs first, then maybe I better see Clifford."

"Is Klaus at his mansion in Beverly Hills?"

"No, he's been staying at a desert chateau near the Springs," she answered. "We've transferred some of the completed weapons and ships there by truck."

"Yeah, that's what Hix must've seen."

"Hix knows about this? You promised me you—"

"Darn, there I go again, being loyal to my own kind. A bad habit I'll have to shake."

"Damn you, I do love you," she said in a loud voice. "Don't you think it would be a hell of a lot easier for me if I didn't?"

"Torn between love and duty," he said. "I've written about that, too. Once I got two cents a word for it."

"You're acting like a—"

"Hate to cut off youse lovebirds, but I got to move." June was sitting up, eyes glassy, in the back seat. She held a ray gun in her hand.

Pete said, "Where'd you get that thing, June?"

"I ain't June at the moment," she said in a harsh voice. "I been using dis bimbo's mind for quite a while now—takin' it over an' livin' in it when I needed it."

Tracy said, "Roscoe Muldow."

"In person."

"You're one of them. I should have suspected. You're from Peregrine."

"Not only dat, sister, I am da boss of da whole shootin' match. And now . . ."

Zzzzzummmmm!

22

"Yik-yik!"

Something prickly was rasping at his cheek.

"Yik-yik!"

Something furry was wrapping around his neck.

"Toko, you little prick. Where are you?"

Pete became aware of the sun. It was directly above him, burning at his eyelids.

Opening his eyes he saw a chimpanzee grinning at him, smelled strong banana breath.

"Hey, Toko," Pete mumbled, "it sure is nice to see you."

"Yik-yik!" The movie monkey gave him an enthusiastic hug as he sat up.

"Toko, can't I even get out of the car by the side of the road to take a piss without you . . . Holy shit!"

An enormous man with shaggy hair and in a white suit came running over to him, buttoning his fly. It was Hunneker, the jungle king.

"What are you doing flat on your ass next to that cactus, buddy?"

"Think I got dumped out of a car," Pete answered.

"Yik-yik!" Toko planted a kiss on Pete's forehead.

"Son of a gun—he really seems to like you." Shooing the chimp off, Hunneker bent and helped Pete to his feet. "He usually hates most people and likes to take nips out of them. Only person besides me he gives a shit for is a girl named Tracy Flinn."

"I'm a friend of Tracy's. Toko and I have met before." He almost fell when the jungle man let go of him.

"Easy now, pal," said Hunneker, putting a beefy arm around Pete's shoulders. "Small world, huh? Running into a pal of Tracy's. I was on my way to the Springs from Nevada. Been doing a little gambling and wick-dipping," explained Hunneker. "Stopped at what looked to be a lonely spot to pull John and then this putz goes scampering off on me."

"I appreciate his finding me."

"You get rolled or what?"

"It's more complicated."

Flat desert stretched away on both sides of the straight and level highway. Hunneker's parked crimson Duesenberg was the only car anywhere in sight.

"I'll give you a lift," said Hunneker. "If somebody hooked your car, the Highway Patrol can—"

"No, this isn't exactly in their area," he said. "Look, you've got to take me to the *Skyrocket Steele* location. It's about ten miles outside the Springs."

Hunneker scowled. "Well, I got a sort of heavy date in town."

"Tracy's in trouble."

"*Yik-yik!*" Toko grabbed Hunneker's thumb and forefinger and tugged.

The jungle man shrugged. "Hell, if it's for Tracy, we'll sure do it. Knock that off, Toko."

The chimpanzee abandoned his master's hand and climbed into Pete's arms. "*Yik-yik!*" He commenced examining Pete's hair.

"That little putz really likes you." Hunneker helped Pete into the passenger seat of the car. "Do snakes bother you?"

"I haven't met enough to be sure. Why?"

"Got a batch of them in that basket there next to you on the seat."

"I'll try to get along."

"*Yik-yik!*" Toko whacked the lid of the basket with a hairy fist.

"Leave those guys alone, putz." Hunneker squeezed in behind the steering wheel. "What sort of trouble is Tracy in?"

"Big," said Pete, "I'm afraid."

"She's a nice kid." The car roared back onto the road. "You got something going with her?"

"Something."

"She at the location? That why you got to get there?"

"No, she's probably somewhere else—somewhere in the vicinity of Clifford Klaus," said Pete. "I'm hoping to pick up something I need first."

"I'd tag along and help," said Hunneker, "except I got this date."

"*Yik-yik!*" said Toko.

23

"Wish I had time to stick around," said Hunneker. "This looks damn interesting."

"Thanks for the lift." Disentangling himself from the affectionate chimpanzee and scrambling out of the Duesenberg without overturning the basket of snakes, Pete stood on the desert road for a few seconds gazing at the smoldering ruin of one of the prop warehouses.

It was nothing but a tumbledown crosshatch of charred beams and twisted metal sheeting.

"There better be something left in the other one." He started to run for the second warehouse, which seemed to be intact.

Before he reached it a voice ordered, "Stop right there, young fella."

A grim-faced man of fifty was moving toward him through the scatter of milling crewpeople. The midday sun made his sheriffs badge flash on his narrow khaki chest.

Pete said, "I really don't have time to—"

"First off, who might you be?"

"Pete Tinsley. But, look, I have—"

"Hold on a minute now." From a hip pocket the sheriff withdrew a small spiral-bound notebook. He began turning its pages one by one. "Yessir, here you are. 'Peter Tinsley, age twenty-eight, tall and good-looking, sandy hair.' Well sir, I wouldn't exactly go along with the good-looking part, although, being sheriff of Manzana, I see an awful lot of movie folks and so my standards might—"

"Can you tell me what's been going on here?"

"Wellsir, a fella name of . . . Just a sec while I look it up. Fella name of Hix telephoned that he'd been knocked out by gangsters and tossed in a clump of cactus. Then these so-called gangsters abducted . . . let's see . . . 'June Maze, blond hair, pleasing figure, age about twenty-five or -six and a . . . Oh, yeah . . . a Miss Tracy Flinn. Spelled F-L-I-N-N. Described as being—"

"I already know that part," cut in Pete. "How come the damn warehouse burned down?"

"Wellsir, I can explain that, more or less." The sheriff turned a few more pages. "Seems there was some kind of raid, led by . . . Here's his name . . . Roscoe Mudlark . . . Nope, that's Muldow. Yep, Roscoe Muldow . . . You know, there are times I can't read my own—"

"Where's Hix? Was he seriously—"

"Hix? Oh, the fuzzy-headed fella. Last time I saw him he was—"

"Pietro, my boy, where in blue blazes have you been? And where are the ladies?" Hix, head swathed in too much gauze, came trotting across the sand toward them. "We've had a busy night."

"Tracy or June didn't come back here, did they?" Pete asked him.

"No. Aren't they with you?"

"Tracy was most likely taken to—"

"Seems like, Mr. Tanksley, that you know more about this than—"

"Hix, what exactly went on?"

"You mean in addition to the daring midnight kidnapping?"

"I'm more interested in the fire."

"Well, right after I put in my call to Sheriff Winship to report the snatching of you three, I heard a fresh commotion," said Hix. "I got over here in time to see spaceships flying out of that warehouse. A crew, led by none other than Roscoe Muldow, was loading ray guns and such into waiting trucks. Some of the cast and crew tried to stop 'em but got zapped with the ray guns. Curly Horner's still stiff as a board over in his cabin, and Bud Duttlinger says he's all prickly in the legs. Anyway, a couple of big cars come roar-assing up. Out pops Milton Owls and Thompson, along with a squad of heavies who were complete and total strangers to me. After which all hell breaks loose, a pitched battle ensues, and Roscoe's gang seems to get a mite discouraged. Pedro, both sides of the frumus are using some very unearthly weapons and then Roscoe whips out a real doozy of a gun. He uses it on Milt and Thompson." Hix swallowed, rubbed both hands through his frazzled hair. "Pete, as Allah is my witness, both Milt and Thomps turned right to dust. Dust. I tried to show Sheriff Winship which little pile was Milton and which was Thompson, but he—"

"You Hollywood fellas are crazier than I figured if you think I'm going to swallow a cock-and-bull story like—"

"It's true, every word," swore Hix. "Even the fertile Hix brain couldn't concoct the likes of what happened here last night, sheriff."

"There's going to be a showdown," said Pete, taking Hix by the arm. "Or, damn, it may have taken place already. Do you know where Clifford Klaus's desert hideaway is?"

His partner pointed to the south. "Thataway. Klaus bought a castle sort of setup from a crazed old millionaire prospector name of Salt Flats Eli a couple of years back. What's that got to do with any—"

"Sheriff, you're going to have to excuse us now."

"Excuse you? Dang, this Hix fella is my key witness, even if he is slightly goofy."

"No more time to talk." Running, urging Hix along, he headed for the still-standing warehouse. "Let's just hope they left something."

"I get the impression more than national defense is involved," said Hix.

Letting go of him, Pete tugged the sliding corrugated metal door aside. "Hey, great! We can use one of the ships."

Three silvery rocket ships remained inside the domed building.

Pete hurried to the nearest. "I'm assuming these have been activated, since they were going to move them out to Klaus's."

"Activated?" Hix blinked.

Sheriff Winship caught up with them. He stood undecided on the threshold of the warehouse, calling in, "What the devil is all this here?"

Ignoring him, Pete got the door of the spaceship yanked open. "C'mon, Hix, we have to find out how to fly this damn thing."

"We're going to fly somewhere?"

"Over to Klaus' place." Pete climbed up into the cabin. "I think that's where they'll all be. This morning Roscoe overheard Tracy telling me that's where the rest of the weapons are stockpiled."

"We're alluding to the selfsame Roscoe who was here this A.M. turning our boss into grit?"

"It's a knack he has for being more than one place at the same time. I'll explain later."

"Yes, do."

Pete settled into the pilot seat. "If this works anything like an airplane, we're in business."

"You know how to fly a plane?"

"I've sold seven short stories and four novelettes to *Stimulating Air Stories.*"

"Oh, grand, that fills me with confidence." Hix, gingerly, took the seat next to him.

"Say in there! You better come on out right away," shouted the annoyed sheriff through the open door of the spaceship cabin.

"How about this one?" Pete pushed a dash panel lever ahead.

There was a woosh and the door slammed shut in the face of Sheriff Winship.

"Very good," said Hix, grinning. "Do something else."

"I think maybe this switch here ought to start the engines," said Pete as he flipped a red switch.

He was right.

24

"Zowie, this is terrific!" exclaimed Hix. "More exciting than the last chapter of *The Masked Pilot Flies Again,* and that caused seventeen heart attacks in the Midwest alone." The fuzzy-haired writer had his face pressed to a round window.

They were flying over the desert at an altitude of five hundred feet, wobbling some, lurching now and then. The rocket ship's engines were incredibly quiet; the speed indicator registered a rate of two hundred miles an hour.

Pete, hunched at the controls, said, "What about those ray guns?"

"Don't you feel euphoric and full of oomph?" Hix cocked his head to watch the sky rush by. "We're in a genuine spaceship, me lad, just like Skyrocket Steele and associates. Hellsfire, we're the first Earthmen ever to do such a thing. That makes up pioneers."

"Yeah, it's awesome," agreed Pete. "But at the rate we're traveling we'll be at the castle in minutes. I want to be prepared."

"Ah, that early Boy Scout training left its scars on you." Leaving the window, Hix knelt on the cabin floor beside a metal box he'd found in the rear compartment of their rocket ship. "I note two different sorts of shooting implements herein, Pedro. Beats me, however, how one tells if they're activated."

"Pull the trigger."

"All well and good if fate puts a stunner in my mitt," said Hix, nose close to the large deep box. "Should I pick a duster, we'll end up with more northern exposure than we need."

"There's nothing lethal in there. Tracy swore to me that all their weapons were designed to—"

"Would this be the same Miss Flinn who informed you Clifford Klaus was so patriotic he went around sporting a little white beard and a star-spangled topper?" inquired Hix. "Klaus then turned out to be from such a remote spot in the galaxy that it'd cost twenty-six dollars and change just to send him a postal card or—"

"I know what the stun-ray gun looks like—Dangler used one on me."

"Okay, okay." Hix scooped a gun from the box and crossed the cabin. He held it up near Pete's eyes. "This?"

"No, it's got a longer barrel and a fatter stock."

"Coming up, boss." Hix made his way back to the box, traded the gun for a different model. "This him?"

"Yeah, looks like."

Putting a finger to his ear, Hix held the ray gun out at arm's length and aimed at the wall of the cabin. "I feel like Prof Avon on a bad day," he said, and pulled the trigger.

Zzuzummmmmm!

When the beam hit the wall the metal made a faint pocking sound.

"Seems to be in working order," said Pete.

"I'm not cut out for this war-of-the-worlds life. Shooting this thing off gave me a toothache." Keeping the weapon at arm's length, Hix deposited it on the floor beside the box. "From what you've told me about this interplanetary feud we're about to muscle in on, Petrov, we may never get a chance to land this crate. I just bet these Esmeraldans and Perigrinates have some positively spiffy antiaircraft guns."

"The ship I saw them use back at the studio had built-in guns, too, I'm pretty sure." Pete was watching the blank desert unfold below them. "See if we do."

"They really ought to have sought my advice before naming sides in this brawl." Hix, pressing his palm against the curving metal wall of the cabin, worked his way to the door leading into the rear compartment of the rocket. "Esmeraldans isn't too nifty a tag, nor is Peregrinians. Sounds like, that last one, a little Armenian restaurant in Glendale. Come to Peregrinian's for swell food. Give me a robust name, like the Brooklyn Dodgers, the Purple Gang, the—"

"We'll be there any minute."

"Excuse my girlish prattle, admiral." He ducked into the rear of the ship. "It's simply that I've never been part of one of my own serials before. Living the life of Skyrocket Steele is . . . spooky."

"We've arrived," Pete called out. "And things don't look so hot."

Hix bounded to a rear window. "Yoicks, I agree!"

There was the sprawling sandstone castle up ahead on the hazy desert. It stood in a small valley between low scrubby hills, towers and spires jagged and gaping now, swirling streams of black smoke climbing up from it into the afternoon. Circling over the besieged castle were three mammoth spaceships, and each one was shooting beams of purplish light out of its glistening sliver underside. The wreckage of another five ships was scattered across the desert around the castle. When a beam managed to connect with the Klaus mansion a great chunk of the structure came toppling away, squirting stones and debris.

"What a terrific scene!" Hix said. "Oh, would that I had James Wong Howe along with me. Or even a midget with a Brownie."

The Esmeraldan forces were returning the fire, shooting rays of purple and crimson up from the fortress.

"Bull's-eye!" hollered Hix.

A stripe of crimson hit one of the circling rocket ships. A full second passed before the entire craft went exploding away across the smoky sky. It was like a giant jigsaw going to pieces—great ragged hunks of silvery fuselage, flapping shreds of cable, thousands of slivers of glass and metal—all rushing away from each other. And men—remnants of them—went pinwheeling through the air.

"Where's Tracy!" muttered Pete. "Jesus, where is she?"

"They ought to label things in this ray-gun nest," complained Hix from the rear cabin. "'This is your death ray, this is your freeze ray.' You know, the way things are done in a Pullman. 'Don't flush while in the station' and other helpful hints."

"Ray guns ought to be standard equipment—keep looking."

Shortly Hix appeared in the doorway to announce, "I do believe I have located the dornick which works the guns. Any time you wish to give it the old school try, just yell. Do you see any sign of Tracy or June?"

"Just a minute." Pete managed to get their rocket ship to climb.

When they were above the two Peregrinian-staffed spaceships, he set the controls for what he hoped would be a circling pattern.

Hix stationed himself at a circular window near the copilot

seat. "Aha, there's a white roadster which well might've been owned by a dapper underworld figure," he pointed out. "See it? Parked in amongst those yucca trees on the little bluff to your right."

"That's the car, yeah," said Pete, excited. "Look —that must be Tracy and June next to it on the ground."

"'Tis, yes. They're spread out on the sand," said Hix, squinting. "Only unconscious I'll wager, since even from this height I can see Juney's impressive bosom heaving."

"There's a pickup truck parked near them in the brush."

"Indeed," agreed Hix. "The lout sitting on the running board is either Lionel Stander or our very own Roscoe Muldow. My vote goes to the latter."

"It's Roscoe, sure enough. What's that he's got hooked up to him?"

"Radio gear, my boy. Our little chum is no doubt calling the plays from that vantage point, telling his goons in the borrowed spaceships what to do. A common practice of generals."

"I'm going to try to land near them."

"Oops," blurted Hix. "The Peregrine team has realized we ain't reinforcements. One of them ships is coming up to give us the once-over." He went sprinting back to the gun compartment.

Pete took back the controls. "Could be these guys can even sense we're not on their side."

The curious rocket ship was zooming up toward them. In the cabin were two men in coveralls.

"Hold on," advised Pete.

He guided their ship into a bank to the left.

"Yikes! This reminds me of a hangover I enjoyed once in San Pedro."

"Damn!"

Somehow the Peregrinians were now above them, moving into a splendid position to fire down.

"Try some diversionary flying," suggested Hix. "That's what the Masked Pilot would do in a fix like this."

Struggling with the controls, Pete nosed the ship down and then put it into a slow loop.

Zzzzzzillle!

"They're shooting at us, Pedro."

"I noticed."

They continued their loop.

"Whoopee! I got 'em in what I think are the gun sights!"

Zzzzzzilllle!

Their ship was traveling, belly up, beneath the other craft.

A shock wave from an immense explosion hit them.

"Yreka!" yelled Hix. "A hit!"

The remains of the Peregrine spaceship were spilling across the sky.

A huge fragment of ruptured metal wall slammed into their side.

Pete was trying to level out. He found he couldn't.

Their rocketship wobbled along upside down, then abruptly spun over upright.

An odd ratcheting sound was spilling up out of the control panel, thin swirls of greenish smoke were coming from some-place unseen. The ship commenced dropping toward the ground. They were rushing toward the desert.

Hix said, "If this is your idea of how to land this buggy, I—"

25

Hix came crawling across the slanting floor of the cabin. "I think we survived the crash," he observed. "Unless this is one of those highbrow dramas in which we're all dead and headed for heaven in a rocket."

Pete became aware something—most likely his own blood—was trickling down across his face. When he tried to wipe at it with his right hand, he discovered his arm was broken. "Hix, I seem to have—"

The door to the cabin all at once shrieked and came slamming open.

It hit the rising Hix full in the chest, sent him stumbling back into the rear compartment again.

"Youse guys better be dead in here!" roared Roscoe Muldow as he struggled to climb into the smoky, tilted cabin. "Otherwise I'm gonna kill youse all!"

Getting himself free of the pilot seat, Pete threw his body to the metal floor. He landed on his right arm and only by biting down hard did he keep from crying out in pain.

He used his knees and his left elbow to propel himself across the floor to the box of guns.

"Ain't no crumbums gonna screw up da Peregrinian cause!" Grunting, the thickset Roscoe was pulling himself into the rocket ship. He had one ray gun stuffed into his belt, another gripped in his fist.

The ray gun Hix had set aside had gone sliding away someplace during the crash. No time to hunt. Pete grabbed a fresh one from the box.

"Get back, Muldow!" he warned. His voice sounded very whiny and kidlike to him.

"Like hell, youse greenhorn!" He lunged into the metal room, gun swinging up to fire.

Zzzzzatttzzz!

Pete shot first.

The beam dug into Roscoe's wide chest. The man gave out a mewing scream, then began to disintegrate. It was as though the bright sunlight outside was trying to push its way through his body. He became less and less substantial; the light showed through the growing gaps in him. His body crackled, rasped, turned to dust along with his clothes and weapons. He became a rough lumpy caricature of a man, then lost even that semblance to life. He collapsed in on himself, became only a pile of dust on the metal flooring.

"Good Christ," said Pete, sick, swallowing hard. "I got . . . I got the wrong kind of gun."

"He was going to knock us both off." Hix came stumbling out of the gun cabin.

"Yeah, I know, but—"

"Look, I just killed off a ship loaded with guys I never even met," his partner said. "So maybe I'm no better than some Luftwaffe bastard who strafes a line of refugees. Be that as it may, I feel nifty about being alive and kicking."

Pete edged to the doorway. The light desert wind was already working at the remains of Roscoe Muldow, scattering them. Taking a deep breath, he leaped over the dust and out into the desert. His arm was throbbing, his stomach full of pains that tried to double him up.

Their rocket ship had crashed on the far side of the bluff where the roadster was parked.

"Lean on me, chum," offered Hix, catching up with him.

Pete put his left arm around Hix' shoulders. "Tracy ought to be uphill here."

"June as well," said Hix. "Now that Roscoe is defunct, I figure her mind, such as it is, will be her own again. She's no Boots, but with my true love in far-off Hollywood—"

"I really thought I'd grabbed a stun ray, Hix. I didn't even know the other type of gun would do what—"

"Over and done," said Hix. "Going to take some time to get used to, but . . . Good golly!"

A huge pillar of fire came roaring out of the side of the last spaceship. It had been hit. After wavering in a lopsided arc, it went plummeting straight into the castle.

The grating crash was followed by a small explosion, a larger one, and another.

"Time to hit the deck." Hix aided Pete into a flat-out pose on the sandy slope, joined him.

More explosions came, each stronger than the last. The aftershocks sent great gusts of smoky air rolling down over them, plus grit and tatters of brush.

After a quiet minute or two, Hix said, "That seems to be the end of the fireworks display, junior." He raised his fuzzy head in a tentative way, spitting out sand. "My, but this has been one of those days. Law me, I can hardly wait to get back to the plantation and jot the day's events down in my keepsake book."

With an assist, Pete got to his feet. "They had weapons and explosives stored in the damn place." He started trudging up the hill.

"A safe assumption." Hix continued to shed grit. "I am also entertaining the suspicion the forces of Esmeralda and the forces of Peregrine have succeeded in canceling each other out. An apt little lesson on the follies of war."

As best he could, Pete started running. He'd seen Tracy—the girl was conscious and kneeling beside the reviving June. "Tracy," he called.

She was crying when she stood up to face him. "Everyone's gone," she said. "I can sense that. I'm all alone."

"Not completely." Pete put his good arm around her.

Hix crested the hill. "If this were a movie, I'd end it right here," he said. "Give 'em a nice clinch and no time to wonder whether or not there's going to be a happy ever after."

THE END